THE GIRL FROM YESTERDAY

Robert Ashton and Kate Gibson are a month away from their wedding. However, Robert's ex-wife Caroline turns up from Australia with a teenage daughter, Karen, who Robert knew nothing about. Then, as Caroline and Robert spend time together, they still seem to have feelings for one another, despite the fact that Jim, back in Australia, has asked Caroline to marry him. Now, Robert and Caroline must decide whether their futures lie with each other — or with Kate and Jim.

TERESA ASHBY

THE GIRL FROM YESTERDAY

Complete and Unabridged

LINFORD
Leicester

First published in Great Britain in 1982

First Linford Edition
published 2013

British Library CIP Data

Ashby, Teresa.
  The girl from yesterday.- -
(Linford romance library)
1. Love stories.
2. Large type books.
I. Title II. Series
823.9′2–dc23

ISBN 978–1–4448–1394–4

Published by
F. A. Thorpe (Publishing)
Anstey, Leicestershire

Set by Words & Graphics Ltd.
Anstey, Leicestershire
Printed and bound in Great Britain by
T. J. International Ltd., Padstow, Cornwall

1

Robert Ashton took a drink from his glass without taking his eyes from the pub door. He was a good-looking man in his mid-thirties, but the tension he felt showed clearly in his expression.

The pub was fairly busy, and he'd deliberately chosen a seat which would give him a reasonably uninterrupted view of the entrance.

One or two people recognised him and nodded in his direction, but it was not one of his usual haunts and most of the patrons were strangers to him.

Companionable by nature, he felt conspicuous sitting there alone. He was nervous, too, as, over and over, he asked himself, what am I doing here? Why did I ever agree to meet her . . . ?

The door opened suddenly and he half rose to his feet as an attractive woman walked in.

Too young, Robert thought as he sat down again. But it was so long since he'd seen her. How would she look now? She was bound to have changed, he thought, as the question sprang into his mind yet again — what exactly did Caroline want with him after all this time?

Surely it was more than just looking him up for old times' sake. What had she said — something important to tell him . . .

And what would Kate, his fiancée, make of all this? He hadn't mentioned this meeting to her at all, but with good reason.

They were to be married in a month and here he was, nervously waiting to meet another woman . . .

*　*　*

Caroline had been cryptic on the phone when she'd called out of the blue a couple of days before. She'd given no hint of why she wanted to meet him, saying only that it was vital they did.

His curiosity had been aroused, but Caroline had insisted that she needed to speak to him face to face. Whatever she had to say couldn't be said over the phone.

Again the door opened, along with a rush of cold air. This woman was the right age — blonde, in her mid-thirties, but she didn't look tall enough. Maybe, though, just maybe —

As the woman caught his eye and smiled, he made to get to his feet. Then, embarrassed, he sank back into his seat as she was joined by her partner, who cast a suspicious glance in Robert's direction.

Grinning sheepishly, Robert looked away. He closed his eyes for a moment trying to picture Caroline as she'd been the last time he'd seen her.

Tall, slim, with blonde, shoulder-length hair and dark-blue eyes. One thing was certain — he'd always been proud to be seen with her. She'd liked to look good and he guessed she'd still take pride in her appearance.

The sound of the door opening again caught his attention and he looked up.

This time he didn't jump to his feet. He was rooted to the spot as he looked at the tall, elegant woman in the doorway. He knew instantly, beyond any doubt, that this was Caroline — this was his ex-wife.

The woman paused, looking around for a moment as heads turned in her direction. Robert rose to his feet to greet her.

'Robert!' Her face lit up in a smile when she saw him moving towards her. How could he ever have worried about not recognising her?

'Caroline!' He took her arm and somehow the gesture turned into an awkward embrace as he brushed his lips against her cheek in greeting. 'You — you look marvellous,' he murmured, leading her over to the table. 'Have a seat,' he said. 'I'll get you a drink. Do you still like wine?' He was aware of talking quickly to cover his uneasiness.

She nodded happily. 'White wine will be fine, Bob, thanks.'

When he came back, it seemed simple and natural to slip into a conversation about the past. It was almost as if the intervening years hadn't happened as they chatted easily about old times.

'Hey, I noticed the Rialto's been turned into a bingo hall!' Caroline exclaimed, shaking her head in surprised disbelief. 'I passed it in the taxi on the way here. We used to see some great films there, didn't we, Bob.'

'We did. Except when we were in the back row!' he joked. 'Anyway, I bet that short drive brought back lots of memories.'

'It certainly did,' she said dreamily. 'I saw the old cafe, too — it's been turned into a hairdressing salon! Remember how we'd sit all night with just two coffees? Yet the owner — Don, wasn't it — never grumbled.'

'That's right. Don was a gem. He was never going to get rich on what we spent, was he?' Robert remembered. 'He's still around, but he gave up the cafe years ago because of heart trouble.'

'Ah, that's a shame,' Caroline sounded genuinely sorry and Robert took a moment to look at her while she was absorbed in her own memories . . .

★ ★ ★

There were a few fine lines around her eyes now, but they only seemed to add to her attractiveness. Her features had more character these days. She was still a very beautiful woman.

Glancing round the pub, Robert could see Caroline was attracting quite a few admiring glances, but that was hardly surprising.

With her healthy, Australian tan and gleaming, blonde hair, she looked stunning.

Caroline leaned across the table and touched his arm, breaking into his thoughts.

With her startling blue eyes fixed

upon him, he was reminded of how she used to make him feel — as if he were the only other person on earth when he was with her.

'You know, in those days, Bob, I only had eyes for you.'

He looked away, embarrassed at her frankness. But he sensed her staring at him and realised she was waiting for him to respond.

'I guess we both thought it was the real thing in those days,' Robert answered softly. 'But we must have been mad, getting married at seventeen. We didn't stand much of a chance really, did we?'

Caroline laughed softly. 'No — all the odds were stacked against us. We were madly in love, but we had no idea of what real life was about.'

She leaned back in her chair, her expression tender now.

'It was inevitable that we'd end up going our separate ways, Bob. I'm sure of that.'

Robert felt a pang of sadness

somewhere deep inside, but at the same time, he knew she was probably right. They'd been young, impulsive, so sure of themselves, but it hadn't been enough.

The cramped flat they'd lived in had been intended as a stop-gap until they could afford the house of their dreams.

But after the first few weeks, the rows had started. At first these had been followed by wonderful reconciliations, but eventually the silences had become prolonged and making up lost its passion.

'So,' Caroline broke into his thoughts, 'what have you been up to over the years? Did you end up working with cars? That's what you always wanted, wasn't it?'

He nodded, feeling instantly more at ease talking about his lifetime fascination.

'I've got a couple of garages of my own now,' he told her proudly, realising suddenly how important Caroline's approval of his success was to him.

She looked genuinely pleased. 'That's marvellous, Bob. You've done really well for yourself. I'm glad.'

Flattered by her interest, Robert continued, 'And now I even have enough time on my hands to indulge in my hobby!'

'Vintage cars?' Caroline guessed. 'You were always crazy about them.' She laughed infectiously and clapped her hands.

'Right!' He grinned boyishly.

'And, Bob, I've just remembered — you were always keen on wildlife and nature — '

'Still am — and I'm off into the wilds whenever I get the chance. How about you?' Robert countered. 'Is Australia really the land of golden opportunity?'

Caroline laughed again. 'Well, if you've enough determination and ambition it is — yes, I guess it is. It's worked for me anyway. In the past few years I've built up my own interior design company. We're doing pretty well.'

'You always did have a flair for colour

and design,' Robert said enthusiastically. 'It sounds perfect for you.'

'I love it.' Her eyes shone as she talked about her work. 'I get contracts from all over the place. I've just finished some designs for a new hotel complex in Fiji, and a Japanese company has been showing an interest. I do private homes, too. If they can afford me!' She smiled, eyes shining with amusement.

'But seriously, it's great to do something you really enjoy. It's not like working at all and now that I have a partner, I can take some time off, knowing the company's in safe hands.'

For a moment, her eyes took on a faraway expression as if her mind were back in Australia.

It had all happened so long ago now, but Robert would never forget how he'd felt when she told him she was going to emigrate with her parents to far-off Australia.

Although he hadn't really wanted to lose her, he'd also known, deep down, that they couldn't go on as they were and that it was better to part friends.

So, less than a year after they'd walked down the aisle, filled with love, hope and expectation, he'd found himself waving her off at Heathrow Airport, relieved, but sad, too, certain that he'd never see her again.

'You look very content, Bob,' Caroline said quietly, interrupting his thoughts. She eyed him thoughtfully. 'Is there a special lady in your life — or am I prying?'

For the first time since Caroline's arrival, Robert allowed himself to think of Kate, and immediately his face softened.

Caroline was surprised to see the sudden change in him.

'No — no I don't mind telling you,' he said softly. 'There is a very special lady. In fact, we're going to be married in a month's time.'

'That's terrific!' Smiling, Caroline reached across the table to take his hand. 'I'm so happy for you, really I am. Who knows, maybe I'll be as lucky one of these days.'

As Robert covered her hand with his, he could see something was troubling her. She had walked into the pub exuding confidence and self-assurance, but now that veneer seemed to be slipping.

It was almost as though the news of his forthcoming marriage had had something to do with her sudden change of mood.

'Look, Bob,' she said earnestly, lowering her eyes as she spoke, 'I asked you to meet me for a reason, not just to talk about old times.'

Robert felt his heart thudding in anticipation.

'Remember when I called you the other day, I said I had something important to tell you?' She swallowed hard and the colour seemed to drain from her face.

'I'm afraid there's no easy way of saying this, so I'm going to come straight out with it.'

'Go on,' he said softly, 'I'm listening . . .'

2

'Women!' Andrew Gibson muttered, flopping down in an easy chair in his comfortable sitting room. 'What a way to spend a morning, Sam!'

Sam, his elderly, black Labrador, settled down beside him, gazing expectantly up at his master.

'You were better off here, Sam,' Andrew continued, patting him consolingly. 'Believe me!'

He sighed with relief. Then, loosening his tie, he leaned back and closed his eyes, resting his hand on the dog's soft head.

Andrew was a pleasant, youthful-looking man in his late forties. He'd been engaged all morning as a chauffeur-cum-lackey for his daughter, Kate, and her bridesmaid and best friend, Marie.

It seemed he'd spent hours trailing

around department stores behind them, weighed down by bulky carrier bags. He'd no idea a bride would require so many 'necessities' for a wedding.

But, he reminded himself, he had volunteered to help, and so he had only himself to blame.

Now they were upstairs, Kate and Marie, trying things on. Their laughter drifted down to him and he smiled to himself, glad that his daughter was so happy.

'Listen to that racket, Sam,' he said, rubbing the dog's ears affectionately.

After a time, Andrew rose to his feet and stretched. Sam was up, too, wagging his tail expectantly.

'Not yet, Sam. We'll go out later. I've plenty of work to be getting on with first,' Andrew said wearily as he moved across the room and sat down at his ancient writing desk. Sam settled down at his feet.

He hadn't written more than a couple of lines when he paused, pressed the pen against his lips and looked at his own wedding photograph sitting on his desk.

Putting the pen down, he picked up the photograph and looked at it wistfully.

Alice had been so young, so beautiful on their wedding day, and she would have been so proud of Kate. If only she could be here now to see her daughter married . . .

She'd have liked Robert, too, he was sure of that. In fact, he thought with a wry smile, he couldn't imagine any woman not liking Robert!

* * *

Kate had been seven when her mother had died, but she'd handled the situation admirably. She'd been so brave, and so loving and helpful towards Andrew as she grew up.

It was as if she'd tried extra hard to please him and now here she was, a lovely, young woman — a dedicated, primary school teacher — about to be married to a man Andrew held in high regard. Despite his initial reservations about the age gap between them, he knew they were perfectly suited.

With a sigh, he gently placed the photograph where he could still see it clearly. He missed Alice so much sometimes, even though she'd been gone so long now.

Kate and Marie were still in high spirits and, even as he picked up his pen again, Andrew knew he wouldn't get any work done with all the distractions going on around him.

He glanced at his watch and realised that it was almost time for him to visit old Mrs Petrie in the old folk's home in the next village.

'Come on then, Sam, let's go.' He stood up and pulled on his shoes. Then he took the dog's lead from the peg and fastened it to Sam's collar.

'Kate,' he yelled up the stairs. 'Kate, I'm going out!'

'Hi, Dad!'

Kate peered sheepishly at him over

the banisters and he thought how lovely his daughter looked — raven-haired, and with a gentle beauty just like her mother.

'Sorry — were we being too noisy for you to work?'

'Yes, you were, young lady!' he replied, chuckling, as he headed for the front door. 'I'm just off to see Mrs Petrie. So I don't know when I'll be back, love. You know how much she enjoys a good natter.'

'Hold on, Dad!' Kate called, rushing down the stairs to his side.

She reached up and smoothed out his lapels, before kissing his cheek.

Her tone was chastising as she brushed some of Sam's hairs from his coat. 'Dad, where's your dog collar?'

He grinned at her, his eyes twinkling. 'The only one wearing one of those round here today is Sam!' he replied. 'Now I'm off. I'll see you later. 'Bye, love.'

'Give Mrs Petrie my love,' Kate called as he hurried out of the vicarage.

Kate bounded back upstairs and into her bedroom where Marie was struggling with a hooped petticoat.

'I'll never get used to this thing!' she complained, standing up and holding out her hands in despair.

'But you know your dress needs something to give it shape!' Kate laughed at her friend. 'Anyone would think you didn't want to be my bridesmaid!' she added impishly.

'What?' Marie exclaimed. 'After all that shopping I've helped you to do? I've got blisters on my blisters!'

'I just can't believe this is actually happening.' Kate sat down on the bed, her eyes shining. 'Only a month to go,' she said excitedly, 'before the big day!'

'So it is,' Marie agreed, slipping the hooped petticoat off before bouncing down on the bed beside Kate.

'And Robert's not bad looking — for an older man, that is!'

She fell backwards with a shriek of laughter as Kate tossed a cushion at her.

'You're just jealous!' Kate giggled. 'He's the best-looking guy for miles around — and he chose me!'

'What do you mean he chose you?' Marie snorted disdainfully. 'As I recall, it was you who chased him! The poor man didn't stand a chance,' she teased. 'I would never have believed you could be so brazen, Kate!'

'OK, OK,' Kate conceded. 'Well, so what if I did chase him a bit? I'm not too proud to admit it! I fell for Robert the first time I saw him — when he was helping Dad restore that old Morris Minor of his.'

'And he didn't stand a chance after you set out to nail him!'

'It wasn't like that!' Kate smiled and rolled on to her stomach. 'We just seemed to hit it off right away. Mind you, I did make a point of being around whenever he came to work on Dad's old car.'

'And you the vicar's daughter, too!'

Unperturbed, Kate went on. 'Then he asked me out to dinner — '

'And the rest, as they say, is history!' Marie interrupted, grinning. 'All the same, I never thought you'd end up with the local Casanova, Kate!'

'Robert's not like that!' Kate sat up, immediately on the defensive. 'OK, he's had a few — a lot — of girlfriends. But he just hadn't found the right one until I came along. He was waiting for me!'

Kate's eyes became serious then. 'Honestly, Marie, I've never felt this way about any other man. I don't even mind about him having been married all those years ago.'

Marie realised Kate was being serious.

'Don't you really?' she asked gently.

'It was just a crazy teenage marriage that should never have been,' Kate said assuredly. 'It was doomed from the start.'

Marie looked closely at Kate. Her friend's obvious happiness was infectious.

'But our marriage is bound to succeed,' Kate was saying with real conviction.

'I love him so much, Marie. I won't ever let anything come between us . . .'

* * *

Harriet Simpson closed the file she'd been looking at and placed it on her desk. Then she smiled as she heard familiar footsteps coming along the corridor towards her office in the old folk's home where she was matron.

Quickly, she straightened up her cap and checked her appearance in the mirror.

There was a tap on the door and Harriet looked up eagerly as Andrew Gibson popped his head round.

'Hello, there.' He smiled, eyes twinkling. 'All right if I pop along, now, to see Mrs Petrie, Harriet?'

'Of course! She's expecting you,' Harriet replied warmly. Andrew and Sam were always welcome visitors at the home.

Harriet came around the desk and stroked Sam's head. Then, taking a biscuit from her pocket, she slipped it into the dog's mouth.

'You spoil that dog,' Andrew admonished with a smile.

'He deserves it, Andrew. All our residents love to see him. Maybe he's even more popular than his master!' She laughed lightly. 'Look, how about joining me for a coffee before you leave?'

'Sounds great,' he replied, easily. 'See you later then.'

* * *

Mrs Petrie looked frail propped up against several, snowy-white pillows, but her eyes lit up as soon as she saw Andrew approaching.

Andrew knew how much she looked forward to his weekly visit and so he made sure he never let her down. He'd known her for a long time, and her late husband, too.

'Oh, you've brought Sam along,' Mrs Petrie cried, reaching out to stroke the dog. Her eyes sparkled with pleasure. 'How lovely to see you both!'

Sam wagged his tail furiously, thoroughly enjoying all the attention.

Mrs Petrie had once owned a Labrador called Digby who'd been her close companion after her husband's death.

'It's good of you to give up so much time to come to see me,' Mrs Petrie went on. 'I know how busy you are, Andrew.'

'It's no bother, Mrs P. I always enjoy talking to you,' Andrew told her, his natural charm coming to the fore. 'And I've never forgotten how much you and Mr Petrie encouraged me when I was starting out in the parish.'

They shared a brief, companionable silence, as fond memories filled their thoughts.

'And how are all the wedding preparations going?' Mrs Petrie asked at last.

Andrew groaned. 'That daughter of mine . . . She's worn me out! We must have been in every shop in town this morning!'

Mrs Petrie leaned across and patted his hand. 'Oh, well, be patient, Andrew. She'll be full of the joys at this time. Now then — ' She leaned over and began to fumble in her locker drawer.

'Can I help?' Andrew offered.

'It's all right, I can manage,' she told him. 'I know what I'm looking for. Ah, here we are!' She struggled to sit upright again.

Andrew watched as, carefully, she unfolded a cream, silk and lace handkerchief, her old fingers trembling slightly as she fumbled to spread it out on the bed. At last, there, nestling inside, Andrew saw a tiny, gold locket.

'That's a beautiful piece of jewellery,' he remarked appreciatively.

'It's very old. Do you think Kate will like it?' she asked hesitantly.

'It's for Kate? But, Mrs Petrie, you can't — '

'Now don't argue with me, Andrew Gibson!' she said firmly. 'I've made up my mind, and you know how stubborn I am once I've made up my mind! I'd like Kate to have it.'

'It's exquisite,' he breathed, folding the handkerchief gently back around the locket. 'I'm sure Kate will love it. You're too kind . . . '

'I had a long and happy marriage, Andrew, and I like to think that the locket brought me luck in love. I hope it'll do the same for your Kate.' Mrs Petrie smiled sweetly.

'She might like to wear it on her wedding day,' Mrs Petrie suggested. 'Something old and all that — it's traditional.'

'I'm sure she will,' Andrew said, softly. 'Thank you very much.' He leaned forward and kissed her cheek. 'I'm very touched.'

He rose to his feet. 'And now I must be off. I promised Matron I'd drop in for coffee on my way out — mustn't keep another lovely lady waiting! See you next week, Mrs P.'

After he'd gone, Mrs Petrie settled

back against her pillows, musing over Andrew's visit. Once Kate was married, he was going to need someone to look after him.

She had never thought of herself as a matchmaker before, but if she had learned one thing in her long life, it was that happiness can be elusive.

She'd have to make sure that it didn't slip past Andrew and Harriet . . .

3

Kate set her coffee mug down on the table and flopped into the big armchair by the window. She closed her eyes for a moment, savouring the warm, spring sunshine.

Her friend, Marie, had gone home and she was enjoying the quiet moment when the doorbell rang.

She groaned softly at being disturbed. Then, presuming it was someone on church business, she went to answer the door.

'Robert!' she cried in delight. 'What a lovely surprise. Hello, darling!'

She ushered him into the hall and kissed him full on the lips.

'Come through — I've just made some coffee. We've been so busy today. You wouldn't believe it.' Kate positively bubbled with happiness.

'I've been to the florist and organised

all the floral arrangements and that new store in the High Street actually had exactly the shoes I wanted.'

Robert followed her through to the kitchen, watching her carefully as she poured the coffee, but barely hearing a word she said as she chattered on excitedly.

'They're really nice — quite high so you won't tower over me in church! I'll probably trip down the aisle with them, though!'

Picking up his mug, she carried it through to the lounge. Silently, he followed her.

'Oh, and a couple more presents have arrived — gorgeous towels from the Goughs and a beautiful silver tray from Mr and Mrs Everson. Everyone's being so kind!'

She put his coffee down beside hers, looking lovingly at him as he stood hesitantly in the doorway. Then, suddenly, for the first time, she realised that something was wrong. He looked strained and his eyes were dark.

'What's happened, darling?' she asked anxiously. 'Have you had a bad day at the garage?'

'No — no, it isn't anything like that.' He came into the room then and sat down on the sofa.

Kate sat down beside him, putting her arm around his shoulders.

'What's wrong, darling?' she said gently. 'What is it? Tell me.'

Her happy mood was beginning to ebb. Her joy at seeing Robert unexpectedly was tempered, now, with doubt. What on earth could have happened to make him so tense and odd all of a sudden?

'You're not suffering from pre-wedding nerves or anything, are you?' She laughed nervously, attempting to make light of the situation.

He looked at her then, but his smile was forced. 'This is so difficult. I just don't know where to begin.'

Kate's heart sank. Had he changed his mind about getting married? He put his arms round her as if to reassure her, but she could feel his body tense.

'Maybe when you hear what I have to tell you, you won't want to marry me.'

'Nothing could be that bad,' Kate said, her voice husky with emotion. 'Nothing could make me change my mind, you know that.'

He took a deep breath and clenched his hands so hard that his knuckles shone white.

'I got a phone call a couple of days ago — from Caroline, my ex-wife. She's here, in England.'

Kate gasped. She'd always thought that, since Caroline was in Australia, she was out of Robert's life for ever and could never pose any kind of threat.

'Why?' she said shakily, at last. 'Why is she here now? And — and why did she get in touch with you?'

'I was as surprised as you at first,' he admitted. 'She said she wanted to see me and so we arranged to meet for a drink.'

'Robert, I don't understand — why?' She was trying hard to stay calm.

'Well, I thought it was just for old times' sake, you know, but she sounded a bit odd. Then she said she had some vitally important news, which she couldn't tell me about over the phone.'

Downcast, Kate stared at him. She had a sinking feeling that everything she'd hoped for and dreamed of was about to come tumbling down around her.

'I didn't tell you, darling, because I didn't want to upset you. Anyway, I wanted to find out what she had to say. Believe me — '

'I do believe you,' Kate said earnestly. 'But what did she want? She's obviously upset you somehow.'

He gripped her hands tightly in his, searching her eyes with his own.

'Kate, there's no easy way to tell you this — and I only found out myself today . . . ' He sighed and concern was etched all over his face.

'Apparently, when Caroline left for Australia all those years ago, she was pregnant. Kate, I have a daughter.'

'A daughter!' Kate tore her eyes away from Robert's anguished face feeling a numbing sense of dismay.

'I can't believe it,' she said at last. 'Robert, I don't know what to say. How can you have a child and not know?'

She looked straight at him, her troubled eyes demanding some kind of explanation.

'I didn't know, Kate — that's the truth. I had no idea Caroline was pregnant when she left for Australia.'

Kate could only stare at him in disbelief.

'And how is all this going to affect us?' she asked calmly, even though she was trembling inside. 'We're supposed to be getting married in a month, Robert. Now, well, you've got new commitments, I suppose.'

'Kate.' Taking her hands in his, Robert tried to draw her towards him to comfort and reassure her.

But she wrenched her hands free and pulled away from him, deliberately putting a distance between them. Right now his touch was more than she could bear.

'Look, Kate, what can I say? I'm sorry this — '

'Sorry! What good's sorry?' she cried. 'Robert, how do you expect me to feel?'

'It was a shock for me, too, you know,' he admitted. 'When I got that call from Caroline, I'd no idea what she wanted to see me about.

'Believe me, Kate, none of this alters the way I feel about you. I still want to marry you — and it won't affect the wedding plans at all, unless — unless you've changed your mind.'

She shrugged, her eyes still troubled.

Her voice was shaking. 'I — I just don't know how I feel any more, Robert. You can't expect me to behave as if nothing's happened.

'Anyway,' she said, and tossed back her mass of dark hair, meeting his eyes defiantly, 'how can you be sure the child is yours? And why has your ex-wife waited all these years before contacting you?' She paused for a moment while he thought this over.

'I don't know, Kate. I honestly don't know — '

He looked so confused she felt a sudden need to comfort him, but she quickly checked the urge.

'It isn't like that, Kate,' he said at last. 'Karen just wants to meet me. It's only natural for a kid to be curious about the father she's never seen.'

'A kid?' Kate looked aghast. 'But she must be — seventeen. She's almost as old as me!'

'Take it easy, Kate, please,' he reasoned. 'I know it's a terrible shock for you. I'm still trying to get used to the idea myself. But what do you expect me to do? Do you want me to ignore the fact that I have a daughter? Pretend she doesn't exist? Kate, please, try to see it from my side, darling. I have to see her. She's part of me — my flesh and blood.'

Kate took a deep breath, trying to make sense of her feelings as they spun out of control in her mind.

'That means you'll be seeing Caroline again,' she flashed angrily, unable to hide her hurt even though she realised now that Robert was just as bewildered as she was.

'Well, she is the girl's mother after all. Look, Kate, I know how upset you must be feeling. It's strange for me, too, seeing Caroline again. But nothing will change between us. It's you I love — will always love, you know that.

'Caroline and I happened a long time ago now,' he continued almost desperately. 'I'm glad she's doing well, but that's all I feel for her, Kate — the kind of warmth friendship brings, nothing more.'

But instead of smiling and coming to him as he had expected her to do, Kate deliberately turned her back on him, arms folded before her.

Bleakly she stared out of the window, aware of him watching her. Her own reflection rippled before her eyes, an image of misery and disappointment that nothing could ease.

Only a few hours ago, she had felt on top of the world. Now it was like the beginning of a nightmare . . .

* * *

'All set for the do tonight then, Mrs Petrie?' Sophie Jones, one of the young auxiliaries in the old folk's home asked teasingly, as she brought the old lady a cup of tea.

Despite her frailty, Mrs Petrie laughed infectiously at the young girl's remark. 'I'm a bit past all that, dear!'

Sophie then switched her attention to Harriet Simpson, the matron of the home.

'How about you, matron — you going to the dance? After all, it was your idea.'

Harriet looked a little tense, but managed a smile.

'Er — no, Sophie. I don't think so. I've got rather a lot to do with going on holiday soon.' She straightened slightly, brightening a little.

'But I'm sure it will be a success — we've already raised a fair bit of cash from the ticket sales. With the raffle and a few other fund raisers that have been organised, we might even be able to stretch to a second-hand mini-bus. We'll just have to wait and see.

'Anyway be sure to enjoy yourselves,' she added breezily before moving away.

'A mini-bus!' Jan, another nurse, exclaimed. 'That'll mean mystery tours, trips to the seaside and goodness knows what else. There'll be no stopping us!'

'I thought it was supposed to be for trips into town, hospital visits and so on,' Sophie pointed out.

'Don't be so boring!' Jan laughed. 'We could do with a bit of fun round here, isn't that right, Mrs Petrie.'

'Count me in for the beach trip!' Mrs Petrie joked in reply.

Then she glanced across to where Harriet was arranging some spring flowers in a vase and couldn't help noticing the sadness in the matron's eyes.

'Why won't you go to the dance?' Mrs Petrie demanded later as Harriet came across to plump up the cushions at her back.

'I've too much to do,' Harriet began, then with an exasperated smile, admitted, 'Well, actually, I've no-one to go with, and I just don't like turning up at functions on my own.'

'But you said — '

'Not another word, Mrs Petrie,' Harriet said warningly. 'Here comes the vicar.'

With a quick smile at Andrew, Harriet went back to arranging her flowers.

Mrs Petrie shook her head sadly. It was so sad that a caring, attractive woman like Harriet should be lonely. And she was lonely, there was no mistaking that.

'Well,' Andrew said, beaming, 'How's my favourite lady feeling today? I must say, you're looking very bright this morning, Mrs P.'

'Oh, I don't do too badly for an

antique!' Mrs Petrie chuckled and leaned forward to stroke Sam. The dog gazed up at her with his gentle, liquid eyes and she felt better for just seeing him.

'Seriously, Andrew,' she went on, 'I don't regret moving here one bit. It was the best thing I ever did. Everyone's so pleasant.'

Andrew agreed. 'It's certainly got a nice, friendly atmosphere.'

'How about you, Andrew?' Mrs Petrie said suddenly. 'You don't seem quite your usual jolly self. Nothing wrong, I hope?'

Andrew was annoyed with himself for letting his feelings show. But since Kate had dropped her bombshell earlier about Robert having a daughter, he'd hardly thought of anything else. To think of Robert as a father — and of a teenage girl! He shook his head. He still couldn't take it in.

But what was worse, what troubled him more than anything, was his daughter's apparent inability to cope with the situation. She was very young and, he supposed, too idealistic.

Andrew stroked his chin thoughtfully. If he knew Robert as well as he thought he did, his future son-in-law would want to meet this crisis head on.

'Oh, it's nothing for you to upset yourself over, Mrs Petrie,' he said eventually. He tried to sound optimistic. 'There's a slight hitch with the wedding arrangements, that's all. Nothing that can't be sorted out, though, I'm sure,' he added breezily.

But could it be sorted out in time? He couldn't get Kate's unhappy face out of his mind. When she'd told him about Robert's daughter, she'd obviously been feeling upset and hurt. He forced himself back to the present as Mrs Petrie continued talking.

'You mustn't worry yourself about Kate,' the old lady was saying consolingly. 'She's got a good head on her shoulders. No, it's you I'm concerned about, Andrew.'

'Me?' He laughed in surprise. 'Why

on earth should you be concerned about me, Mrs Petrie?'

'Well, once Kate's married, and you're on your own, you'll miss her, you know. She's been your whole life up to now.'

'That's true.' He nodded. 'But I'll survive. I've always got my work and my garden — and I've got Sam!'

Instinctively, Andrew patted the dog's head. 'He's all the company I need and, besides, he doesn't argue with me!'

Mrs Petrie's eyes narrowed. 'Well, I know if I were thirty years younger and a handsome chap like you was footloose and fancy free, I wouldn't be letting you stay by yourself with just a dog for company. Believe me, Andrew Gibson,' she continued sternly, 'it's a wife that you need, not a dog!'

'Don't be daft!' Andrew burst out laughing, forgetting his problems for a moment. 'Who'd have an old fogey like me?'

'Well,' Mrs Petrie announced, 'I happen to know of a very attractive woman who isn't a million miles away!'

Her eyes strayed towards the far end of the room, where Harriet sat, chatting to another resident.

It was such an obvious gesture that Andrew had to stifle another laugh.

'And you'll know, of course, about the dance tonight,' she prattled on. 'You will be attending, won't you? And would you believe that, as yet, Harriet doesn't have a partner? So, you'd better be quick off the mark before someone else asks her.'

She gave her friend an encouraging nudge. 'Well, Andrew Gibson, what are you waiting for?' She gave him another little prod and he detected a wicked twinkle in her eye.

'OK, Mrs P.' He laughed and got to his feet. 'I get your drift. See you next time.'

Mrs Petrie smiled to herself and gave a satisfied sigh as she watched him walk out of sight with Sam trotting at his heels. Since her husband's death, she

42

knew only too well what it was like to be lonely.

* * *

Mrs Petrie dozed in the chair and opened her eyes to see Harriet coming towards her, a wide smile on her gentle face.

'I really don't know whether to thank you, or give you a jolly good telling off!' Harriet shook her head. 'I thought you should be the first to know that I'm going to the dance with Andrew Gibson! And I suspect it's got rather a lot to do with you.'

'Are you, dear?' Mrs Petrie asked innocently and nodded her approval. 'Well, that's nice, I am pleased for you. You both work so hard and it's good to relax sometimes . . . '

4

Kate glanced at Robert as she got into the car beside him and her heart lurched as she noticed how attractive he looked in his dark suit. Yet she couldn't check the feelings of anger and disappointment she felt. Maybe it was simple jealousy on her part — but it still hurt.

She stared right ahead at the road, wishing she was anywhere but here.

'I shouldn't be coming,' she whispered as he started the engine.

'Well, I think you should,' he replied quickly, his expression tense as he turned to look at her. 'You're my fiancée, after all! I need you with me, Kate. I'm a nervous wreck just thinking about this meeting.

'Try to see it from my point of view, will you, darling? All this time, thousands of miles away, I've had a child

— and I had no idea that she existed. Can you even begin to imagine what that feels like?'

His expression softened. 'I'm weeks away from marrying the woman of my dreams when, out of the blue, I discover I have a daughter. Not a child, Kate, but a young woman.'

'I know that, Robert, but — '

'Remember, Karen's bound to be nervous, too, darling.'

Trying to push her nagging doubts aside, Kate smiled longingly at him as he put the car into gear and drove off.

Robert glanced sideways at her. 'Caroline's looking forward to meeting you.'

Kate's heart sank. Of course — his ex-wife, Caroline, would be there, too! After all, she was the girl's mother! She thought Robert seemed nervous and excited at the same time.

'There's the restaurant now,' he murmured, turning into the carpark. 'We're a little early.'

He looked at Kate as he switched off

the engine and caught her troubled look. He reached out to take her hand. 'C'mon Kate, just remember that it's important to me that you're with me here.'

He gave her a small kiss. 'You coming tonight means a lot to me. You mean everything to me, sweetheart.'

Kate managed a quivering smile.

'Ready now?' Robert gave her hand a final, encouraging squeeze and smiled the heart-stopping smile she'd fallen in love with. 'I'm scared stiff, too. We'll just have to give each other moral support!'

They walked into the restaurant. 'They're not here yet,' he remarked.

Kate was aware of him watching the door from where they stood and felt more and more like an intruder, although she had to admit to feeling more than a little curious. Suddenly, Robert got to his feet. Beside him Kate tensed.

She stared at the tall, elegant woman who had just come through the door, and her stomach turned somersaults. So this was Caroline! This beautiful, stunning blonde had once been Robert's wife.

As she walked towards them, Caroline seemed to exude confidence and self-assurance.

She was quite unhurried, as if meeting an ex-husband and presenting him with a daughter was an everyday occurrence.

If Caroline was feeling at all nervous, then it didn't show. Kate could only smile weakly in response.

And, as if one shock wasn't enough, Kate's thoughts cartwheeled yet again as Karen walked in behind her mother. Kate stared from Robert to the girl and instantly there was no longer any doubt in her mind that Karen was, indeed, his daughter.

With that rich, dark hair and those stunning blue eyes — for she was as dark as Caroline was blonde — she couldn't not be his child.

Kate was acutely aware that beside

her, Robert was so delighted at this first glimpse of his daughter that he was virtually floating on air.

'Hello, Caroline, you found the place OK then?' He was speaking to his ex-wife, but Kate noticed that he could hardly tear his eyes away from his daughter.

'It wasn't too difficult, Bob.' Caroline smiled. 'This must be your fiancée?'

'Oh, yes, Kate, I'm sorry. I'm forgetting my manners. This is Caroline.'

'Hi. Nice to meet you, Kate.' Caroline's eyes sparkled, then she turned to the tall, dark-haired young girl who was hanging back a little uncertainly.

'Bob, this is Karen — your daughter. Karen, meet your dad.'

'Hello, Karen. It's great to meet you.' Robert beamed. 'This has to be the biggest surprise of my life! Mind you, this is all a bit weird to say the least, but now I've seen you, I know I've done something right in my life!'

They all laughed as the ice was broken — except for Kate.

At once she was aware of the chemistry between Karen and Robert — an instant bonding between father and daughter, something which excluded everyone else in the restaurant.

'I'm really glad to meet you, too,' Karen breathed excitedly. 'It's a dream come true for me, only better! I've thought of this so many times and now it's happened. I just can't believe it.'

The necessary introductions over, they moved towards their table, Kate walking with Caroline as Robert and Karen led the way.

They were so alike, it was incredible. And the emerging confidence and style of her mother was apparent in Karen, too.

It came as a shock to realise she could see both Robert and Caroline in the girl. This was their daughter — she, Kate, did not belong with them.

'I can hardly believe it,' Robert said as they took their places at the table.

Kate noticed he was no longer stunned and anxious looking — he was beginning to relax now, obviously proud and happy to have met his daughter.

'So you and Robert and getting married next month?' Caroline remarked conversationally, bringing Kate out of her confused thoughts. She saw that the other woman was smiling warmly.

Kate nodded distractedly.

'Yes, that's right.' But her eyes were drawn again and again to Karen and Robert and she could tell from the girl's expression that she was completely captivated as she gazed adoringly at her father.

Obviously Karen's dreams had been realised, just as Kate's had been shattered.

The charged, electrifying atmosphere began to dissipate as Karen now spoke again in her soft, Australian accent.

'I can't believe it's true,' she said. 'I'm finally sitting here with my dad! We have so much to catch up on, don't we?' Her excitement was infectious. 'And you don't look any different from your photographs!' she added cheekily.

Robert grinned at the compliment. 'Flatterer!' Then he became serious again.

'We've seventeen years to catch up on, Karen,' he added quietly. 'I'm just glad of this chance.'

'Well, if it's OK with you, I'd like to spend some time with you,' Karen went on brightly. 'You know, doing things together, getting to know each other better.'

'Of course.' Robert looked delighted. 'That would be great.'

Karen beamed. 'It's really strange, but I feel as though I've always known you — not as if we've only just met at all!'

Karen glanced at Caroline who was watching the touching scene happily. Kate felt she had no place here. She was sure if she slipped away, no-one would notice.

'So, tell me — what sort of things do

you get up to in Australia? Surfing, swimming, barbecues, that sort of thing?'

'Yeah — sure.' Karen grinned. 'That sort of thing's OK, but what I really like is going out in the bush.'

'You're kidding!' Robert said in amazement, looking at each of the women in turn. 'You must have inherited that from me. Didn't your mum tell you? I'm mad keen on all aspects of nature and the countryside. In fact, there are lots of interesting places I could show you around here if you like.'

'Fantastic!' Karen said enthusiastically.

'There's an old World War II air base over by the marshes which has gone completely wild. There are foxes and rabbits there — and a badgers' set. I stumbled across it by accident.'

'Oh, I'd love to see a real badger,' Karen exclaimed. 'They're so rare, aren't they?'

'Well, around here they seem to be,'

Robert agreed. 'Baiters are the main problem, so those of us who are interested try to keep their whereabouts quiet.'

Kate held her breath. She and Robert had discovered the set together and had vowed to keep it a closely-guarded secret.

'I'll take you to see it if you like,' Robert said softly, leaving Kate feeling instantly betrayed.

It was there that Robert had asked her to marry him — and now he was proposing to take this stranger there, this person he had known all of five minutes!

Feeling Caroline's eyes on her, Kate turned and looked at the older woman. Was that look in her eyes sympathy?

'It looks as though we're on our own tonight, Kate,' Caroline remarked softly as Robert and Karen got their heads even closer together.

Caroline felt a rush of compassion for Kate. This must be so difficult for her. She was very young, younger than

Caroline had been expecting — only a few years older than Karen really.

Caroline tried her best to make her feel part of things.

'When exactly is the wedding, Kate?' she asked brightly.

'In a month,' Kate answered briskly.

'I expect you'll be up to your eyes organising things? It's such a hectic time, the final run-up to the big day.'

'Yes, I am.' Kate's voice sounded clipped even to her own ears. So, to try to appear less difficult, she added, 'Dad helps a lot, but Robert and I have still had a fair bit to arrange ourselves.'

'From what he told me, Robert seems to get on really well with your father,' Caroline said. 'That's nice. I suppose being close to your dad, you can understand why Karen was so eager to meet Robert. She's wanted to come to England ever since she was quite small, but lately she's become quite determined and, well, here we are! I suppose it's all to do with growing up — identity crisis and all that, I guess!'

Caroline shrugged slightly.

'So you see, I had to take a gamble on meeting Robert again, for Karen's sake. I couldn't deny my daughter the chance of meeting her father. It wouldn't really have been fair.'

'Robert told me that you have your own business,' Kate said, finding that, with Caroline's help, she was beginning to unwind a little.

'That's right. But luckily I have a close partner at home. I could confidently leave him in charge while Karen and I came over to England.' Caroline gazed tenderly at her daughter.

Kate was beginning to be aware of something else, too. As well as being beautiful, Caroline was also a very kind and thoughtful person — not the sort of woman she'd imagined at all.

And didn't she say there was someone special back home? Kate hoped so, with all her heart.

And even she couldn't deny that Karen, too, as she talked non-stop about her life and the things she liked to do, was likeable.

All this just served to make Kate feel worse.

Every time she looked at them, they seemed to have moved slightly closer together and the laughter punctuating their conversation flowed freely and naturally. There was nothing forced in their growing intimacy.

There was no doubt about it, Robert loved the girl on sight, just as she loved him.

Blinking back tears, Kate stared fixedly at the floral arrangement in the centre of the table, wishing she hadn't come, knowing more strongly than ever that she didn't belong here, and doubting that she would ever feel that she belonged again . . .

★ ★ ★

Mrs Petrie was sitting alone in the television room, watching an old movie, when Kate appeared beside her.

'Sorry, Mrs Petrie,' she apologised. 'I

didn't mean to startle you. If you're watching the film . . . '

'Not at all, dear.' Mrs Petrie picked up the remote control and switched off the set.

'I wasn't watching at all, just dozing really. Anyway, I've seen that film half a dozen times and it never gets any better.'

'I just came to say thank you,' Kate continued. 'The locket's beautiful and I'll always treasure it.'

'It couldn't go to a nicer person, my dear.' Mrs Petrie smiled and patted Kate's hand. 'My late husband gave it to me . . . ' She smiled, remembering.

'He saved long and hard for it. In fact, it became a symbol of our feelings for each other, Kate. We were very happy together, very lucky — very much in love. That locket means a lot to me and I wanted it to go to someone I cared about. I hope you and Robert will be very happy, dear.'

'Thank you,' Kate whispered, close to tears as she leaned forward to kiss Mrs Petrie's cheek.

It was at moments like these that she realised sadly how much she still missed her mother . . .

The old lady held on to her hand. 'By the way,' she asked casually, 'how did your father enjoy the dance last night?'

'Dance?' Kate looked blank. 'Dad was at a dance? You're joking!' She was still disbelieving.

'Didn't the old rogue tell you he was taking Harriet Simpson?' Mrs Petrie chuckled. 'You know her — she's the matron here and she sings in the church choir. She didn't have a partner to take her and I told your father that he should take her. It would have been a shame for her to miss it.'

Kate looked incredulous.

'Are you telling me that Dad was at a dance — with a woman? Well! Now I think about it, he did say something vague about going out — but not to a dance! I had no idea.' She gasped in pretend horror. 'I thought he was at a church meeting! Just wait till I see him!'

'Oh, leave the poor man alone.' Mrs

Petrie laughed. 'Let him have his little secret!'

Two days had passed since Kate had met Robert's daughter and ex-wife and she was finding it impossible to settle.

Before his precious daughter arrived, she'd either seen him or spoken to him on the phone every day. Now, back from the old folk's home, she glared pointedly at the telephone, but to no avail.

The only reason he hadn't been in touch, she convinced herself, was because he'd simply forgotten she existed!

Sighing unhappily, she moved restlessly over to the window.

'Hello, love,' Andrew Gibson poked his head round the sitting room door, surprised to see his daughter wandering around so aimlessly.

Normally she was so busy, she constantly flitted around the house like a butterfly.

She glanced fondly at her father, taking in the baggy, old cords and the shapeless, fraying cardigan he always wore in the greenhouse.

'I'm going out for an hour or two, love,' he called behind him. 'Are you at a bit of a loose end?'

'I suppose I am, but I don't really feel like doing anything.' She pulled a face.

'Not heard from Robert yet, then?'

'I haven't heard from him since — since the day we met his daughter,' she admitted miserably.

'Look, love,' Andrew said consolingly, 'I'm sure he'll be in touch soon. Remember this is a difficult time for him, too.'

'I know, Dad,' she said tearfully, 'but I can't help thinking he doesn't care any more.'

Andrew frowned.

'Don't be daft, Kate. You know he just has a lot on his mind. Give him a chance, eh? Now will you be all right if I head back to the greenhouse?'

'Yes, of course, Dad. Sorry, I was just being stupid.' Kate smiled. 'Oh, just a moment, I almost forgot! When I went to thank Mrs Petrie for the locket, she was telling me about you and the matron going to a dance together. You didn't say anything to me, you dark horse — '

'Ah — ' Andrew's cheeks coloured but before he could say anything, the doorbell rang. 'Saved by the bell!' He grinned.

'If that's anyone for me,' he added over his shoulder, 'I'm not here — unless it's an emergency, of course!'

Then he hurried out in the direction of the garden.

★ ★ ★

Kate opened the front door and her smile froze. Although she was both pleased and relieved to see Robert, she was determined not to let him off the hook easily. He'd hurt her by not getting in touch and she intended to make him suffer now.

'Oh, it's you, Robert,' she said coolly. 'Nice of you to drop in. Just passing, were you?'

He stepped into the hall and moved to kiss her, but she turned around and went back into the sitting room.

'What's wrong, Kate? Why are you giving me the cold shoulder?' He followed her into the room. 'I've tried to phone several times, but you're never in! I even tried calling you at the school, but you were in a staff meeting. Didn't you get my message?'

'Obviously not. I must say, it's nice of you to spare some time for your fiancée.'

'You know where I've been, Kate.' He was becoming exasperated with her now. 'You know I've been with Karen. It's no secret.'

'Glad you've been enjoying yourself, Robert,' she said sarcastically.

'Kate, it's been a couple of days, that's all. What did you expect me to do? Ignore the girl? Look, she's travelled thousands of miles to see me. I'm her father, for goodness' sake.'

Kate stood in front of him looking angrier than he had ever seen her before. She was normally so mild and easy going that this change in her came as quite a shock.

'I've been taking her around, showing her the places I went to when I was growing up.' His face was set now in a grim expression. 'I thought you'd understand, Kate. Or have you forgotten that Karen's my daughter?'

'Forgotten she's your daughter? How could I? You've told me often enough! The point is, you seem to have forgotten that I'm about to become your wife!'

She held up her hands to keep him away when he moved towards her and he saw flecks of gold glittering in her eyes like tiny balls of fire.

'All right.' She was calmer now. 'I accept she's your daughter and she's here. But she's part of your past, Robert, and I'm supposed to be part of your future. But, frankly, I'm not as certain about our future as I was!'

5

Caroline knew right away that the feet poking out from beneath the car weren't Bob's. Still, as owner of the garage, he'd hardly be likely to be getting his hands dirty these days.

She walked past, the heels of her elegant, suede shoes clicking on the concrete floor as the mechanic slid out from under the car and gave a low whistle.

He grinned and gave her a cheeky wink when she turned to look at him.

'Just wanted to see the owner of those lovely legs!'

'Well, now that you've satisfied your curiosity,' she remarked, enjoying the compliment, 'perhaps you can tell me where I can find Bob?'

'Sure! He's just through the back there.' The young mechanic pointed towards an open door.

'Thanks,' she called, giving him a wave as she walked on.

Once she'd stepped through the open door, Caroline found herself in a large workshop where she could hear a radio playing and someone singing, a little off-key, along to the music.

That's got to be Bob, she thought smiling to herself. Then she stopped as she caught sight of his lean figure bent over the engine of a vintage car.

Her stomach began to flutter as old feelings she'd thought long forgotten rose within her. How she had loved him once . . .

Suddenly he turned around and, surprised at seeing her there, he straightened up, banging his head on the bonnet of the car as he did so. Rather sheepishly, he rubbed the tender spot.

'Caroline, I didn't see you standing there!' He grinned and his face lit up with pleasure. 'What a surprise!' Boy-ishly, he rubbed an oily hand through his hair. 'Have you been here long?'

'I've just got here,' Caroline said 'and

I see you haven't changed a bit, have you?' She smiled.

'Still the same old Bob, up to your ears in axle grease and sump oil! Poor Kate — having to put up with all those filthy clothes!'

Robert gave her a rueful look and shrugged.

'You've even got oil on you nose, Bob!' Caroline took the rag from him and dabbed his nose.

'There — that's better.' She stepped back. 'But, you know, a dirty face always did suit you!'

'Gee, thanks!' Robert pulled a wry face. 'Now, tell me, to what do I owe the pleasure of this visit? Were you just passing by, or did you want to see me about something in particular?'

'Oh, yes!' Caroline suddenly remembered the purpose of her visit. 'Karen asked me to tell you she's sorry she won't be able to make it tonight after all. She said you planned to go walking in the woods — something to do with badgers.'

'That's right.'

Robert turned away and tossed the rag to one side. He was ridiculously disappointed and hadn't realised until now just how much he'd been looking forward to spending this evening with his daughter.

'Never mind.' Caroline sensed his disappointment. 'She's arranged to go to see a rock band somewhere with young Greg — that's my friend, Sue's, eldest son. I think he's get a bit of a crush on her and, well, she didn't want to let him down.'

'Too bad.' Robert shrugged again. 'Still, it's only natural that she'd rather be out with people of her own age than tramping around the countryside with me!'

'They say it's hard for fathers to come to terms with their little girls growing up. I suppose you'll have to face it all in one go, Bob!' Caroline joked.

Robert grinned. Unaccountably he did feel a little jealous as well as disappointed. All too soon, he could lose his daughter to a young man and he'd barely known her five minutes himself!

'C'mon, Bob, there's no need to look so gloomy or to waste this lovely spell of weather. I'm sure Kate will be delighted to go with you.'

Robert pulled a wry face and shook his head. 'She's arranged a gathering of the bridesmaids for final fittings and organising the show of presents and so on. Still, as you say, Caroline, it's a shame to waste this glorious weather. You wouldn't fancy going for a stroll in the country, would you?'

Caroline looked surprised then nodded enthusiastically at Robert's suggestion. 'I'd like that. Bob. I'd like that very much,' she said softly.

* * *

'I'd know those shapely legs anywhere!'

'Hello, Mike!' Kate laughed. 'I thought I recognised those big, flat feet, too!'

'There's no need to be nasty.' Mike slid out from beneath the car and feigned a mournful look. 'You've already broken my heart by falling for my boss!'

'Where is he?' Kate asked, then before Mike could speak, added, 'I know, don't tell me, he's with that other woman in his life, the delectable Dolores!'

The car she had nicknamed Dolores was normally responsible for enticing him away — at least before his daughter had arrived on the scene.

'He's — ' Mike began.

'It's OK.' She smiled. 'I know the way.'

Kate walked quickly through the workshop, but the sound of voices ahead stopped her in her tracks. Robert must be with a customer. She listened more intently, then froze on the spot as she recognised Caroline's soft, Australian accent.

' . . . and what about the wedding plans, Bob? Are they going smoothly?'

Robert sighed. 'I'm not so sure about that,' he confided. 'I've just about had it up to here with this wedding! I'm fed up with all the preparations and all the fuss.'

'Oh, come on, Bob, that's a bit selfish,' Caroline said. 'You've maybe done all this before, but it's the first time for Kate, remember.'

'It's not just that, Caroline. It's, well, Kate's attitude towards Karen isn't exactly helping. I'd hoped she'd have been more understanding about me wanting to spend time with my daughter.' He sighed.

'As it is, she seems almost to resent Karen and begrudges every moment I spend with her — '

'Well, I think you're being a bit hard on her. Finding out about Karen so close to her wedding has thrown her completely. She's got so much to think about anyway — and now this. Most girls have their mums to help. She's bound to be on a short fuse, you know, Bob.'

Robert nodded a little sheepishly.

'I know.' He sighed. 'You're probably right, Caroline. All the same, she's not making things any easier.'

Hurt and dismayed, Kate pressed her back against the wall, desperate not to be discovered. How could Robert talk about her like that — to his ex-wife of all people? The way he was talking he sounded ready to call the whole thing off!

Fighting back the tears, she stumbled back through the workshop and out on to the forecourt. All she wanted was to get away.

Kate turned the corner before the tears began to trickle down her cheeks uncontrollably.

Everything had been so perfect before, she thought miserably. Robert had loved only her. But now Karen — and Caroline — were spoiling everything.

She and Robert were supposed to be getting married in a few weeks and she just didn't know how to handle all this.

Her despair mounted as she thought of how, overnight, she had become the outsider, the one who didn't belong . . .

* * *

Spring, The Reverend Andrew Gibson wrote down, *the time for new beginnings.*

He pressed his pen to his lips and stared up at the sunlight flooding in through the small, stained-glass window of the vestry.

Tiny particles of dust danced hazily before his eyes. He closed them in concentration for a moment.

'Nope — doesn't sound right,' he mumbled, scoring through his words.

He was trying to write his sermon in the peace of the vestry, rather than in his study at home, away from the frantic activity of the final wedding preparations. But, despite the tranquillity, he still found it difficult to concentrate.

Sam, his elderly Labrador, rolled on

to his side, stretched and yawned and observed Andrew briefly through one half-shut eye before settling back down to sleep.

'It's all right for you, lying there in the sun,' Andrew told him, forcing his mind back to the topic of his sermon.

Suddenly it struck him that when Alice had died, he'd found a new spring, as it were, a new beginning, in the church.

He snapped his fingers. That was it! The inspiration he'd been waiting for had come to him at last.

No matter how hard the bad times are, some good always comes out of them . . .

Later, as he re-read his words, he couldn't help recognising a similarity between the subject of his sermon and his personal circumstances.

With Kate leaving home, he was about to embark on a new stage of his life, too.

Sam staggered to his feet and began to nudge Andrew's legs This was a sure sign that he'd been lying still for too long and wanted to go for a stroll.

'You're right,' Andrew said, putting away his papers. 'That's enough for today. Let's take a walk.'

The sun was still warm as it hung in the sky, low and golden, casting a mellow light over the grey church walls.

Andrew paused outside the church for a moment to take it all in. Then, suddenly, the doors of the church hall behind were flung open and a group of women — including Harriet Simpson — surged out.

'Evening, vicar!' one of them called. 'Lovely night. Anyone want a lift?'

Andrew acknowledged them with a wave and a greeting. Then he watched as the group broke up, leaving only Harriet standing there in the twilight.

'Hello, Harriet. How are you?'

'I'm fine, thanks,' she called back. 'As a matter of fact, it's such a lovely evening I'm going to walk back to the home.' She moved towards him.

'I'm glad I've bumped into you,

Andrew,' she said. 'I've been wanting to thank you properly for the other night at the dance. I really enjoyed myself.'

'I'm glad, Harriet, because I did, too,' Andrew assured her, smiling warmly.

Harriet looked away. 'It's all right, you know, Andrew,' she said quickly. 'You don't have to pretend. Look, I know Mrs Petrie had a hand in arranging things but it was very kind of you, all the same.'

He laughed lightly. 'Look, it was my pleasure, despite Mrs P's intervention!'

It was true in a way — he was trying to please Mrs Petrie, but the night of the dance had been one of the most carefree evenings he'd spent in years, and it was all thanks to his attractive companion's sparkling company.

With this disconcerting thought, he glanced away. Since Alice had died, well, he'd hardly even noticed other women and the feelings he was experiencing for Harriet were still too new and unfamiliar for him to handle comfortably.

Deftly he changed the subject to something safer. 'The fund-raising was a great success, wasn't it?'

She smiled in satisfaction.

'Mmm,' she agreed. 'Much better than we'd hoped for.'

The church clock chimed the hour and Harriet spoke again.

'I'll have to dash now, Andrew,' she said apologetically. 'I'm due back on duty at the home. See you in church on Sunday!'

''Night then, Harriet. Nice speaking to you.'

Andrew gazed after her retreating figure before turning, with Sam, towards the little graveyard at the back of the church.

He kneeled down in the soft grass and looked at the simple, white headstone before him.

He and Alice had been so much in love, yet that love had been wiped out so cruelly and abruptly so early on. Despite that, however, he still gave thanks to God. Alice couldn't have left him a more precious legacy than Kate.

She was the one who made his tragic loss bearable.

'Oh, Alice,' he murmured sadly. 'You'd be so proud of our darling, little girl now.'

Even after all the years he'd been on is own — apart from having Kate — he still often felt lonely, missing Alice desperately at times . . .

The pain, the longing, didn't really fade, he thought. He had just learned to cope with it and his faith had been a blessing in that respect. He stopped to rearrange the sweet-smelling flowers in the vase that adorned the grave.

Perhaps it was time now for new beginnings — not just for Kate, but for him, too. New beginnings. Somehow, he knew Alice would approve . . .

6

At the shopping centre in town, Kate looked dispiritedly at the dresses hanging on the rail of the store she was in.

Somehow, she couldn't work up any enthusiasm for this shopping trip. She'd come into town to try to lift her flagging spirits and calm her confused thoughts by buying some clothes for her trousseau — but without success.

Catching a glimpse of her own unhappy face in one of the mirrored pillars, she knew the last thing she wanted her friends to detect tonight was her uncertainty. Everyone would expect her to be bright and cheerful and really excited about her forthcoming wedding to Robert.

But at the moment she was still smarting from the conversation she'd overheard at the garage between Robert and Caroline.

Then suddenly she caught sight of another reflection in the mirror. It was Karen — Robert's daughter! The girl was looking through a rack of jeans.

In her panic to avoid her rival for Robert's affections; Kate tried to slide around to the other side of the pillar, but it was too late. Karen was already pushing her way through the rails of clothes and waving.

'Kate? Is that you, Kate? It's me, Karen. Hold on . . . '

Kate stopped in her tracks and turned round, feigning surprise.

'Oh, Karen, hello! I didn't notice you there,' she said pleasantly. 'What are you up to — buying yourself some new clothes?'

The young girl pulled a face.

'Well, I'm trying to. The problem is, I can't find anything I really like! I'm going to see a rock band tonight with Greg and I want something, you know, cool to wear!'

She smiled, her face open and friendly. 'How about you? What are you buying — stuff for the wedding?'

Kate shrugged. 'Well, I thought I'd have a look for some bits and pieces for my trousseau, but I can't see anything I like either. Anyway I'll have to get back. I'm expecting quite a few people round this evening to see the wedding presents. I thought you were supposed to be going out with your father tonight?'

'Change of plan.' Karen laughed. 'He's taking Mum for a walk instead — because I can't go, you know. Well, look, I'd better dash. 'Bye, Kate. See you soon. Nice talking to you.'

'You, too. Have fun tonight.'

Kate forced her features into a smile and waved as Karen hurried away.

Just where did she go from here, she asked herself numbly as she tried not to think of Caroline and Robert together. Not only was she jealous of his daughter, now she was envious of the time her fiancé spent with his beautiful ex-wife!

* * *

Caroline leaned on the fence and watched the horses in the distance, appreciating the lush, green, rolling countryside she'd left behind so long ago.

'It's so fresh looking,' she breathed, turning to smile at Robert. 'And so English. I've missed all this, you know.'

'Oh, I don't suppose there's a lot you miss really. From what Karen's told me, there's some spectacular scenery around where you live.

'Oh, look . . . ' He caught her arm and pointed across the field. 'It's the fox!' he whispered. 'Look how fast she moves.' He was enthralled.

Caroline's eyes followed the streak of red as the vixen ran across the field, before she disappeared under cover at the far end.

'Pity Karen missed it.' He sighed. 'There'll be other times, though, I hope,' he added, smiling. 'She's a great kid, you've made a really good job of bringing her up, you know.'

'Well, thanks — that's nice of you,'

Caroline replied, genuinely pleased at the compliment.

'And,' he continued, 'I still can't believe how much we have in common. I mean, fancy her loving animals and nature so much, too. It's amazing.'

'No, it isn't. She is your daughter, too,' Caroline said softly. 'She's bound to take after you in some respects.'

'It's just incredible that out of all the bad times we had together, Karen could have happened.'

At these words, Caroline's pleasure was complete. She'd had a few qualms about introducing the girl to her father, but it had all tuned out so much better than she'd ever dreamed — except for Kate's attitude. That had been unfortunate.

A dark shadow overhead caught her attention.

'Quick, what bird's that, Robert?' She pointed up towards the sky. 'Some kind of hawk?'

'Yes, it's a kestrel,' he confirmed knowledgeably. 'There it goes!' Robert cried as the bird suddenly swooped out of the sky. 'It must have seen a mouse.'

'Ugh!' Caroline shuddered and Robert laughed at her.

'Come on,' he said. 'There's a family of swans down on the river. I think they'll appeal to you more.'

They walked until the sun had dipped beneath the horizon, leaving the sky coloured with spectacular streaks of red and yellow.

Caroline's legs began to feel tired and she realised they must have walked miles.

'Bob,' she ventured, 'couldn't we stop somewhere for a drink?'

'Great idea,' he said. 'In fact we passed a nice little pub about half a mile back. Think you could manage to stagger back there?'

Caroline laughed infectiously. 'Just watch me!'

*　　*　　*

'Is it always as crowded as this in here?' Caroline enquired as Robert made his way, with difficulty, across to their table with drinks.

'Not usually,' Robert replied looking around a little perplexed. 'There seem to be more youngsters than usual,' he added. 'Wait a minute — '

He went across to speak to the chap behind the bar. 'Oh, no!' he groaned as he returned to Caroline. 'The local rock group occasionally play here — and they're on tonight! I'm sorry, I'd no idea.'

'So Karen and Greg . . . ' Caroline's words were drowned out by the sudden loud twanging of an electric guitar, followed closely by the raucous singing of a young man in tattered jeans.

Robert leaned closer. 'What was that, Caroline? I can't hear a word — '

'I said, I've a . . . ' Caroline shouted, then shook her head in a gesture of defeat.

Robert stood up, drained his glass and indicated to Caroline to follow him outside. 'Let's go!'

'What a din in there!' Caroline

laughed at her own reaction. 'We must be getting old. I was saying that must be the band Karen and Greg are going to see. They're probably in there somewhere!'

'Well, let's leave them to it — we can't talk in there,' Robert decided. Then he added, 'How about coming back to my place? At least we'll be able to chat in peace there and I can have a good look at those photos you've brought.'

★ ★ ★

Robert came into the lounge waving a bottle.

'This is a good one!' he announced placing two glasses on the table beside Caroline. 'Australian Shiraz — how appropriate.' He grinned.

'How nice!' Caroline's eyes shone. 'This is really very civilised, Bob!'

While Robert opened the bottle, Caroline searched through her bag for the envelope of photographs. Then, handing her a glass, he sat down beside her on the sofa.

She passed the photographs to Robert, watching him closely as he went through them one by one, studying each one avidly. He was obviously intent on taking in as much as he could of his daughter's life. He'd missed out on so much of it.

With every picture, she tried to make Karen's childhood real for him.

'Is this her first day at school?'

'Yes it is.' Caroline sighed and leaned against his arm to get a better look at the picture. 'She looked so tiny and her school uniform was, well, bought to last, I guess! It looks huge on her. Don't you love that one? She looks so grown-up, doesn't she?'

'Oh, Caroline, I wish I'd known her as a child,' Robert said wistfully. 'But thanks for bringing these. Do you think I could have copies made of some of them? Oh, I must have this one . . . '

Finally, Robert laid the photographs down on the coffee table and leaned back, still looking at Caroline.

'Why the sad look?' he asked softly.

'It's nothing — ' Caroline looked away quickly. 'It was just so hard for Karen not having a father like everyone else. I remember her coming out of school that very first day in tears and asking me, 'Where is my daddy?''

Robert felt a lump rise in his throat. 'It must have been so difficult for you, Caroline,' he said gruffly. 'You should have got in touch. I'd have helped — you know that.'

He reached for the wine bottle and when he saw it was empty, he got up to fetch another.

'We've drunk too much already,' Caroline protested lightly, but allowed herself to be persuaded into having another glass of wine.

Robert's arm rested across the back of the sofa.

'You seem to have got it all together now, though,' Robert commented. 'Is there anyone special back in Australia?'

'Well, there is someone special back

home, but I'm not sure how he feels about me.' She gave a shy laugh.

'He'd be mad not to want you.' Robert breathed. 'You're still so very lovely, Caroline.'

He let his arm fall gently cross her shoulders as, almost without thinking, she moved closer to him.

'Remember what you were saying earlier about Karen being the only good thing to come out of our marriage?' Caroline murmured, her voice little more than a whisper. 'Well, that's not strictly true, is it?' Her eyes sparkled flirtatiously.

'We had some awful arguments, I admit that, but we definitely knew how to make up, didn't we, Bob?'

Her face was very close and the light perfume she wore stirred memories Robert had thought long forgotten.

It had been a strange but wonderful evening. They had laughed a lot, been sad together, too, and Robert felt closer to her than he had ever been before.

Light-headed and reckless from the

wine, Robert pulled Caroline closer and she came, willingly, into his embrace.

For a long while, he searched her eyes with his own, seeing in them some of the old fire, the old passion which had once made her so exciting to him — and still did, if he were honest . . .

Deep down, he knew it was time to pull back, to stem these crazy emotions, but it was impossible. Caroline was here, now, in his arms and her lips were only inches away.

As their lips met, the years seemed to fade away and Robert was lost in a downward spiral of memories, which, even as he tried, he could not escape . . .

And as Caroline responded passionately to his kisses, all thoughts of Kate vanished completely from his mind — as if she had never existed . . .

7

Robert still couldn't believe the previous night with Caroline had actually happened . . .

Ever since he'd woken that morning, feeling decidedly hung over, he'd had a terrible sense of foreboding about what had taken place.

And now he desperately needed to see Kate, for reassurance that his future lay with her — and perhaps to alleviate some of the crushing guilt he felt about last night.

It would be easy to blame the situation on having had too much to drink, and the fact that things hadn't been going well between him and Kate, but when it came right down to it, the only one to blame for the previous night's rashness was himself.

It had all been a terrible mistake and when he thought of how hurt Kate would be if she found out, he couldn't bear it.

The ivy-clad vicarage loomed ahead. Expertly he turned into the drive and followed the bumpy road up to the handsome Victorian house where he sat for a moment before getting out of the car. He badly wanted to see Kate, yet how could he face her when he'd behaved so shabbily?

''Morning, Robert. Beautiful day.' Andrew waved from the doorway. 'I saw you coming,' he called. 'Come in, come in! Kate's just up — they had a late night last night!'

For Robert it was hard to return Andrew's open smile and he found himself avoiding his future father-in-law's eyes.

'Hello, Robert.' Kate came through from the living room. She looked a little tired, a little pale. 'I wasn't expecting you this morning. Come and sit down.'

There was no reproach, no sarcasm, but, Robert noted, there was no warmth there, either.

She was being too formal and polite and her father noticed it, too. He decided to leave them to talk and went off to busy himself with church business.

'How did last night go, Kate?' Robert asked awkwardly. 'You look a bit pale. It was a good night, though?'

Surprisingly, the evening had been fun and all the dresses fitted perfectly so there were no last-minute alterations to worry about. Yet her heart had still been heavy.

She just couldn't forget the conversation she'd overheard at the garage. The memory of Robert's thoughtless words to Caroline hurt so much.

Even so, she was determined not to let her feelings show and she certainly wasn't going to bore him with the details of the night before.

'You're sure nothing's wrong?'

Now his voice showed concern and the warm and tender look he gave her almost took her breath away. She gulped.

'No, nothing's wrong.' She smiled back. 'How about you — how did you get on last night?'

'Oh, it was OK, you know.' He shrugged. 'Karen couldn't make it.' His heart was beating madly but he hoped his voice sounded casual. 'So Caroline came for a walk in the country instead. Afterwards we popped into the Feathers for a drink, and she showed me some pictures of Karen as a kid.'

He was taking a gamble, telling Kate that he had been with Caroline, but as long as he didn't make a big deal out of it, surely everything would be all right.

'Sounds nice — I met Karen in town and she mentioned you were going to see Caroline.'

Robert realised, with relief, he'd been right to mention the change of plan.

Again Kate was forcing herself to smile, and she couldn't help thinking that Robert seemed ill-at-ease. Perhaps he was feeling guilty about seeing Caroline.

But surely if there was anything to

hide, he wouldn't have mentioned seeing his ex-wife . . .

'Look, Robert, about the wedding,' Kate began awkwardly. 'I know you must be fed-up with all the fuss — and it must seem to you as if it's all I think about, but — '

'Not at all.' Robert was, in a way, glad of this opportunity to reassure her and even partially salve his own conscience at the same time.

'Look, Kate, it may not look like it, but I really appreciate all the effort you're putting into organising the wedding. I know I should be helping you more — '

Kate smiled, surprised at his sudden change of heart. 'Conscience bothering you, is it?' she teased.

Robert tried to brush off her innocuous remark with a laugh, but his mouth refused to comply.

And Kate knew him well enough to know that there was something else troubling him.

The meeting with his daughter had

gone smoothly and so what could it be now?

She drew a sharp breath. Could it be anything to do with spending last night with Caroline?

Andrew hesitated as he approached the open door of the living room. Looking at his daughter and her fiancé sitting at opposite ends of the sofa, it struck him that they didn't look like a couple who were about to be married.

Robert had seemed a little strange when he'd arrived and Kate was watching Robert staring into space, looking pretty miserable herself.

Andrew drew back, not wanting to pry. Something was wrong here, very wrong indeed.

★ ★ ★

'Oh, it was great, Mum,' Karen enthused. 'This guy played a really brilliant guitar solo and it went on for ever — it was magic.'

Caroline shook her head. How could

her daughter be so bright and cheerful after such a late night?

Caroline felt dreadful. Her head throbbed and her eyes were dry and gritty from lack of sleep.

Her friend, Sue, smiled sympathetically from the other side of the table.

'Your mum's feeling a bit fragile this morning, Karen.' Sue laughed, addressing both her guests. 'Late night, I think. Am I right, Caroline?'

Caroline nodded, barely hearing what Sue said. She was totally absorbed in her own turbulent thoughts.

'Mum.' Karen shook Caroline by the shoulder. 'Are you listening? What were you and Dad up to?' she teased.

'What!' Caroline glanced sharply at her daughter, then realising the remark was innocent enough, relaxed a little.

'You did have a good time with Dad, didn't you?' Karen persisted. 'What time did you get home? I half-expected to find you waiting up for me!'

Caroline closed her eyes. All these questions were making her head spin.

She wished with all her heart that Karen would change the subject.

The telephone rang in the hall.

'It's for you, Caroline.' Sue popped her head round the door excitedly. 'Quickly. It's Jim — in Australia!'

Caroline looked at Karen, then pushed her chair back and hurried into the hall. Sue grinned and handed her the phone.

'Jim, hi!' Caroline was pleased to hear his familiar voice.

'How are you?' Jim sounded relaxed. 'Everything going OK over there?'

'Everything's fine, Jim,' Caroline said happily. 'Karen's getting on really well with her father. How are things with you?'

'It's all going well — nothing I can't handle — for a while, anyway. Caroline, look, the reason I phoned — I'm missing you like mad. When are you coming back home?'

'Oh, Jim.' Caroline laughed nervously.

In her heart she was pleased. Jim had

finally said what she'd been hoping for, but after last night with Bob, she felt torn and confused.

'Jim, it's sweet of you to say it — and I'm missing you, too, but it's Karen. She's still getting to know her dad, and I'm sure she'll want to stay as long as possible. I just don't know when we'll be back.'

'C'mon, Caroline!' Jim's voice had cooled and he sounded exasperated now. 'It's time you thought of yourself for a change. Look — I know I've never told you, but I love you and I want to marry you.'

Caroline gasped at the other end of the line. Jim was proposing to her over the phone!

'Maybe it's time,' he was saying, 'to start thinking about your own future, our future — that's if you feel the same — do you?'

'Jim, I don't know what to say. It's so sudden — and — it's difficult over the phone, to give you an answer.'

'Well, how about giving it some thought,

and, well — if you haven't been in touch by the end of the week . . . '

His voice faded a little and Caroline couldn't help feeling that her big, strong Australian partner sounded more than a little despondent.

' . . . well, then I'll know our relationship is strictly business and I won't push again.'

Caroline put down the telephone, feeling sad and confused. She wanted to go home, to see Jim, for everything to be uncomplicated like it had been before she and Karen came to England.

'How's Jim?' Karen came into the hall.

'Oh, he's fine.' Caroline smiled gently. 'Wonders when we're going home. He's missing me.'

'What?' Karen's face fell. 'Oh, no, Mum! You can't be thinking about going back yet. We've still some time left. I don't want to go home yet!'

Caroline looked away. In her present confused state she didn't know the next step to take — nor in which direction her future lay . . .

8

Several days had gone by since Andrew had first realised all wasn't well between Robert and Kate.

But, at least for tonight, he was determined to put all that out of his mind. This evening Harriet was cooking him a meal.

'Hungry?' Harriet came through from the kitchen. Her face was flushed and she seemed a little nervous.

'I certainly am. Smells great!' Andrew grinned and walked over to open the patio doors. 'You've a lovely garden here, Harriet.'

'Come out and have a look round,' she invited, slipping her arm through his as they stepped out together on to the small patio.

All his worries seemed to melt away as they strolled round the garden. He felt so warm towards Harriet

— protective, somehow, and special.

The dinner Harriet had cooked lived up to the delicious smells which had preceded it. They took their time over each course, chatting as the candles on the table burned low.

And afterwards, as they drank coffee and listened to music, the conversation flowed freely and easily.

When Harriet went into the kitchen to make more coffee, Andrew took the opportunity to glance through Harriet's record collection.

'You have a fantastic selection of music here,' Andrew commented when she returned.

'Thank you.' Harriet smiled. She looked happy and relaxed. 'Anytime you want to borrow anything, feel free.'

Andrew paused and glanced up from the records.

'Actually, there's a classical concert in town next month I was hoping to go to. Would you like to come?'

'A concert? I'd love to, Andrew. I haven't been to a concert for ages.'

'That's settled then. We could even make a day of it! Lunch out, perhaps a boat trip on the river and . . . Listen. I love this bit.'

He closed his eyes as the music changed. 'It's perfect to dance to.' Gently he pulled Harriet to her feet and into his arms.

As they swayed slowly, lost in the gentle music, Harriet marvelled at how relaxed Andrew seemed tonight.

At the fund-raising dance, he'd been a little distant, almost as if he was holding back, but now, as he held her gently, yet firmly, in his arms, she felt as though an invisible barrier between them had been removed.

Andrew could feel himself relaxing, too, the more time he spent with Harriet.

He'd had no intentions of becoming involved with another woman, but now he could no longer deny his ever-increasing feelings for Harriet . . .

Being with her was like being with an old, trusted friend, but at the same time, it felt new and exciting, and Andrew felt strangely bereft when it was time to leave her and go home.

'Thank you for a lovely evening,' he murmured, leaning forward to kiss her cheek. 'Perhaps we can get together a few times — before the concert,' he suggested tentatively.

'I'd like that,' Harriet replied softly, lowering her eyes. ''Night, Andrew,' she said softly, reaching up to kiss him lightly on the cheek. Then she stood at the door, waving until he'd driven out of sight.

Back in the sitting room she put the music that they'd been dancing to back on.

Then she sat down, and closing her eyes, let her mind drift back over one of the happiest evenings she'd spent in a long while . . .

On the way home Andrew sang along with the car radio, his voice rising with his spirits, his mind full of thoughts of Harriet.

Though they had a lot in common,

Harriet had her own opinions, too, which didn't necessarily agree with his — he grinned to himself — that led to some interesting and stimulating conversations.

It was the important things they really seemed to come together on — and that's what mattered, he decided.

He stopped off for petrol and as he got back into the car and opened his wallet to put away his change, he caught sight of the picture of Alice which he always carried with him. Just looking at her he knew she'd be pleased for him.

It was years since he'd felt so good about life, and it was all thanks to Harriet . . .

⋆   ⋆   ⋆

Next morning, Andrew was standing at the study window looking out over the colourful garden, his thoughts still on the pleasant evening he'd spent with

Harriet, when he spotted Robert's treasured, vintage car coming down the road.

He watched as the sleek car turned into the drive and finally glided to a standstill outside the vicarage.

'Nice to see her out and about, Robert,' he remarked, coming out to look over the elegant vehicle.

Running his hands appreciatively over the gleaming paintwork, he commented, 'She really is a beauty, isn't she?'

Unsmiling, Robert climbed out and stood beside Andrew.

'I suppose she is,' he said disinterestedly, and Andrew was amazed to hear him sound so unenthusiastic.

This car was Robert's pride and joy — he'd spent hours restoring it and now, he was regarding it with complete indifference.

'Did you manage to get that part you've been after?' Andrew asked conversationally, in an attempt to raise Robert's spirits.

'Oh, that.' Robert nodded. 'Yes. I had to send to Manchester for it.'

Andrew glanced at Robert. He was staring at the car, a faraway look in his eyes. Something was on his mind, that was obvious — and it wasn't the car.

'She's all ready for the big day then?' Andrew made another attempt at being light-hearted.

When Robert mumbled something incoherent, Andrew guessed that his daughter and her fiancé had not patched up the rift that had developed between them.

If only he could get Robert to confide in him. It must be something to do with Karen . . .

His daughter appearing in his life so soon before the wedding was obviously causing problems.

'Have you time for a coffee?' he asked.

Robert nodded, distractedly.

'OK, Robert, what's wrong?' Andrew asked as they walked into the house. 'Is it Karen?'

'Karen?' Robert swung round to look at him. 'No, Andrew, *my* daughter's not the problem — it's yours. It's Kate!'

Andrew felt his stomach tighten.

Kate hadn't been herself lately, perhaps now he would find out why.

'I just don't know how to put this, Andrew,' Robert went on. 'But I don't think I can go ahead with the wedding, I — '

Andrew stared at him, shocked. Of all the things he'd been expecting to hear, this was the last.

'You'd better come inside,' he said quickly, pushing open the heavy wooden door of the vicarage.

★   ★   ★

An hour later, the coffee stood cold in its cups as Andrew and Robert faced each other, man to man, across the study.

The younger man had told Andrew everything, from Kate's jealousy over Karen, to his own indiscretion with Caroline.

'I know I've let you all down,' Robert said solemnly. 'I can't begin to tell you how ashamed I feel.'

The father in Andrew longed to get hold of Robert and shake him and tell him that he had every right to feel ashamed! But the man in him, the man of faith, held back.

Robert dragged his eyes up to look at Andrew directly. The older man looked uncomfortable.

'I don't blame you for despising me,' Robert said at last. Andrew shook his head.

'I can't condone what you've done, Robert,' he admitted, 'but I can't find it in myself to condemn you either. You've had quite a lot to come to terms with in the past few days. So has Kate.'

'Well, I hate myself,' Robert said angrily, 'for cheating on Kate, for involving you . . .'

'Now, now,' Andrew said as calmly as possible. 'Anger won't achieve anything. You're just feeling sorry for yourself — and you're not the injured party here, are you, Robert?' He stood up, fixing his eyes on the man he had hoped would make his daughter as happy as she deserved.

'There's Caroline to consider, and Karen, too, but at the moment, my first concern is for Kate. And though you may not believe it — for you, too, Robert.'

Andrew turned away from Robert for a moment and looked out of the window, choosing his words carefully when he spoke.

'I haven't always been a vicar, Robert,' he said softly, 'and I don't have a narrow, restricted view of life. I know these things happen. I know real life isn't all happy endings.'

'I wanted a happy ending for Kate,' Robert muttered.

'And so you shall.' Andrew sounded convincing. 'Love, real love, is such a rare and precious thing,' he continued. He was thinking of Kate on the day he'd told her that her mother had died. He couldn't erase the desolate image of her face from his mind.

But Robert's sudden rejection of her, now, so close to her wedding, would cause her real heartbreak and pain possibly even more damaging than losing her mother as a child . . .

'This isn't easy for me, either.' He turned back to face Robert. 'Kate is my daughter and because I love her, I place her happiness above all else. My advice is, don't let what's happened between you and Caroline stand in your way. If you really mean what you said, then put it behind you and concentrate on what lies ahead. The future, yours and Kate's future, is far more important.'

Robert looked up at Andrew, seeing the wisdom in his words, but unsure whether he could live with himself after this, as Kate's husband.

Andrew sensed this dilemma.

'Just tell me this, Robert. Do you love Kate?'

'You know there's no question about that.' Robert bowed his head. 'I'd do anything for her, you know that, Andrew.'

His voice was gruff with emotion.

Andrew took a deep breath. He had to take his own advice now and forget what Robert had just confided in him. It wouldn't be easy, but, for their sakes, he had to try.

'That's all that matters then.' He touched Robert's shoulder. 'It's time for you to look forward, Robert — for us all to look forward. Take my advice and put the past behind you.'

Robert looked up at him, affection and admiration in his eyes for the man who had become such a close and important friend.

Andrew patted him on the shoulder. 'Come on! We've a wedding to arrange. Let's get on with it, shall we?'

*   *   *

It had been dry for so long, that when the rain finally came later that day, it was almost welcome.

'Look at that.' Caroline peered out of the window. 'That's more like the England

111

I know and love. Typical of it to rain when I plan to go into town, though.

'Sure you won't come with me, Karen?'

'I'd rather stay here, Mum, if you don't mind,' Karen said. 'But you enjoy yourself. See you later.'

This was the first time Caroline had driven in England and, after a long spell of dry weather, traces of oil on the road's surface were making it slippery and hazardous.

Confused thoughts of Jim and Bob kept crowding her mind as she tried hard to concentrate.

She hadn't realised she was quite so uptight when she left the house, but it was hardly surprising, and after last night's indiscretion with Bob, and then Jim's ultimatum on the telephone that morning . . .

Suddenly, she felt the steering become light.

The corner seemed to appear from nowhere and her last-minute effort to turn the wheel sent the car into a spin.

She saw the verge coming straight at her before everything went black . . .

⋆ ⋆ ⋆

'Mum?'

'Karen?' Caroline tried to open her eyes, but she felt so weak.

Then as she became more awake, awareness rushed back quickly. She was in pain and for some reason she felt frightened.

'Karen — what's happening?'

'I'm here, Mum.' Karen squeezed her hand. 'It's all right. You're in hospital. There was an accident, but you're going to be OK. We've been waiting for you to wake up. How are you feeling now?'

Caroline forced her eyes open. Things were a little blurred, but her vision soon cleared as she recognised her daughter's pretty face.

'What happened?'

'Don't you remember?' Karen asked anxiously. 'You were in the car. You lost control on that bend just before you turn on to the main road. You were really lucky to get off so lightly, the doctors say. The car's a write-off. And the bad news is you have a broken leg.'

'A broken leg!' Caroline moaned and closed her eyes again.

The door opened and a young nurse came in. She smiled at Karen, then looked down at Caroline. 'Still want to be a rally driver then, do you?'

Caroline responded with a half smile.

'That's better!' Turning to Karen, she said, 'Would you mind leaving us for a moment?'

'Sure.' Karen got up quickly. 'I'll be back in a moment, Mum. I'll pop along to reception and give Dad and Sue a call to let them know you've come round.'

'Just a few things to do,' the nurse told Caroline, bustling around the bed. 'That's good, your blood pressure's coming down. Now your temperature — ' She placed a thermometer in Caroline's mouth removing it after just a few moments.

'How are you feeling?'

'Not too bad — considering what a close shave I seem to have had.'

She looked towards the window and saw that the sun was shining.

'What day is it? How long have I been here?' she asked the nurse.

'Two days, love.'

'Two days! I have to make a phone call.' She tried to sit up but couldn't. 'Please — '

'Not now, love.' The nurse shook her head. 'Maybe later, I'll wheel the phone in for you.'

'But you don't understand,' Caroline cried.

She had intended to call Jim when she returned from the shops. Now he would be convinced that she didn't care for him.

'This is so important,' Caroline pleaded.

The nurse considered for a moment. Finally she sighed.

'I shouldn't be doing this, you know — you're not up to making phone calls yet,' she called over her shoulder as she hurried out of the room. 'I'll be in hot water if anyone finds out!'

Moments later she returned, pushing the phone trolley, crashing it through the door.

'Here you are,' she said helpfully. 'I'll have to dial for you.'

'The number's in my bag,' Caroline said faintly. 'In my address book.'

The nurse dialled the number, then handed her the receiver.

'It's ringing.' She smiled understandingly. 'I'll leave you to it. I'll come back in a few minutes.'

Caroline cradled the receiver to her ear and listened to the regular purr of the ringing tone. It became increasingly jarring and monotonous as it went unanswered. Jim wasn't there.

Too late, she'd realised that her future lay with Jim. It was him she loved and now she'd ruined everything.

Her head felt fuzzy. She dropped the receiver and it hung beside the trolley. She could still hear the persistent ringing.

She knew she should have called him before — maybe now it was too late . . .

9

Caroline watched gloomily from the hospital window for a glimpse of her daughter. Karen and Sue would be coming to collect her soon and somehow before then she had to coax herself into a more cheerful mood.

She should have been pleased at the prospect of getting home, yet nothing lifted her spirits.

She sighed as she stared down at the plaster cast round her broken leg. Of all the times to have a stupid car accident this must surely be the worst. It had ruined everything . . .

Though Karen had coped well, Caroline knew her daughter had been shocked. And what would either of them have done without Sue? Her old friend had been kindness itself — thank goodness they'd been staying with her at the time of the accident.

Somehow she'd make it up to both of them . . .

But how was she to make it up to Jim? That was the worst part of all this. After his sudden proposal over the phone, he'd expected an answer before the end of that week. If he didn't hear he'd presume her answer was, 'No.'

And he hadn't heard — for that had been the week of the accident. Since then she'd phoned Australia every day trying to get through to him, but there as no answer from his number.

Oh, it was all such a mess. She'd been so confused about her feelings for Jim — especially after she'd spent an evening with Bob. But now she knew Jim was the one she really loved — and she'd lost him.

The sound of footsteps in the corridor helped her pull herself together. They were here!

'You're dressed!' Karen breezed into the room and greeted her mother with a hug.

'Karen thought we'd have to help you

get into your clothes,' Sue remarked teasingly.

'Are you sure you're OK, Mum?' Karen's initial happiness had changed to concern. 'You're so pale.'

Caroline smiled weakly.

'I'm fine, really,' she said. 'Just a bit shaky now I'm up and about.'

'All packed and ready to go?' A nurse entered the room, smiling brightly.

'Thanks, Jean.' Caroline smiled warmly at the nurse who'd been so kind and helpful when she'd tried to contact Jim. 'You've been great.'

Sue picked up Caroline's bag and they headed down the corridor.

'You've done really well,' Jean said, encouragingly, walking beside Caroline. 'Just don't go overdoing things once you get home, will you?'

'We'll see to it that she behaves herself!' Sue replied with a grin.

On the journey home, Caroline tried her best to participate in the light-hearted banter between Sue and Karen. It was obvious how much her daughter had missed her, so she made the effort to chat, yet all the time her thoughts kept turning to Jim and what could have been.

She'd even had fleeting doubts about their business partnership. How could they work well together after this?

She'd had her chance and she'd thrown it away, and she only had herself to blame, she thought miserably.

At last they reached Sue's house and Karen helped Caroline out of the car, holding her crutches steady until she was on her feet.

Then she helped her mother make her way slowly up the path and in through the front door before turning.

'Will you be OK now, Mum? I'll nip back and help Sue with the stuff from the boot.'

A little taken aback at what seemed, in her sensitive state, like parental neglect, Caroline made her way laboriously towards the living room. All she wanted to do was to sink into a chair and put her feet up.

The short walk from the car to the house had all but exhausted her.

She paused in the one doorway for a moment to rest, when suddenly she realised that someone was already in the room, a tall, fair figure standing over by the window.

She couldn't believe her eyes — it was Jim!

He was smiling tenderly at her.

'Jim! What a surprise!' Caroline wanted to throw herself recklessly into his arms but circumstances and caution prevented her. He looked so wonderful standing there.

'What are you doing here?' she cried. Tears of delight welled in her eyes.

'What do you think?' Grinning all over his face, he stepped towards her.

Her heart began to pound. She could hardly dare hope that Jim had come all this way for her . . .

'I had to see you, Caroline,' he said simply. His expression was serious. 'And when I got here, I found that you'd had an accident — I'm just so relieved that you're all right!

'I couldn't bear it if anything happened to you,' he added softly. 'I could have kicked myself after I gave you that stupid ultimatum on the phone.'

Suddenly he looked dejected.

'Oh, Jim, I tried to call you so many times — I thought I'd lost you.'

'Never in a million years,' he breathed. Caroline let the crutches slide to the floor. Then she was in his arms and he was kissing her.

'Right after that phone call, I made up my mind to come over here. I couldn't stand being parted from you any longer. I love you, Caroline. I want to marry you. I want to be with you always.' His arms tightened around her.

She turned her face up to his and kissed him long and hard.

'I love you, too, darling,' she said earnestly. 'So very much. And I thought I'd blown it!' She laughed happily.

'I wouldn't have let you go that easily,' he murmured into her hair.

'There's no way I'd have left it to chance, sweetheart.'

* * *

The Reverend Andrew Gibson couldn't contain his pleasure as he stood in the doorway of the sitting room at the vicarage.

What a contrast to the scene he'd witnessed only last week when things between his daughter and her fiancé had obviously been so strained.

Now Robert and Kate were sitting close together on the sofa, oblivious to everything except each other.

Robert's arm was around her shoulders and she was leaning against him, laughing up at him, her eyes shining with love.

It brought a lump to his throat seeing them so happy. It made him feel happy.

As he watched, Kate reached up and touched Robert's face, then he bent his head to kiss her. Quickly, Andrew turned and walked across the hall to the kitchen, closing the door softly behind him.

'I think we'll skip the coffee, Sam, and go for a walk.' He smiled down at the dog. 'This calls for a tactical retreat!'

He grabbed his jacket and opened the back door, breathing in the cool evening air deeply.

Andrew was still smiling to himself as he strode down the path towards the fields at the back of the vicarage.

In two days' time, his daughter would be married and he couldn't think of anyone he'd rather have for a son-in-law than Robert Ashton — although he had to admit it had all looked decidedly unlikely less than a week ago.

But now that all the doubts had been aired and settled, he was looking forward immensely to the wedding.

Sam raced ahead, then, seeing a rabbit hopping along at the edge of the field, took off in pursuit.

* * *

The airport was bustling and crowded and the coffee bar was full of people and their luggage.

Outside, the loud drone of aeroplanes taking off and landing reminded them that it wouldn't be long until the flight to Sydney was called.

Caroline shivered, despite the warmth of the day. Although she was returning to Australia with Jim, Karen had decided to stay on in England a little longer and Caroline was going to miss her dreadfully.

They were very close — closer than many mothers and teenage daughters — possibly because there had only ever been the two of them.

The last thing she'd expected when she'd brought her daughter here a few weeks ago was to be leaving her behind. But she could understand her daughter's reluctance to leave.

There was still so much Karen wanted to see and do in England as well as spending more time with her father.

She also knew, as she watched Karen talking animatedly with Bob, that she was leaving her in caring hands. Although Karen would be staying with Sue, she sensed Robert would make it his business to keep an eye on her.

Even Kate, in her way, was fond of Karen and hopefully one day they'd even become close friends.

'All right, love?' Jim put his arm around her waist and gave her an affectionate squeeze. She looked up at him and saw the concern in his eyes. He knew how hard this parting with her daughter was — even though it might only be temporary.

Kate approached them, smiling warmly.

'It's a pity you and Jim couldn't stay for the wedding,' she said, then impulsively, she kissed Caroline's cheek.

'I'm not sure that would have been the right thing to do, Kate,' Caroline said quickly. 'Besides, with a business to run back home we can't both be away too long.'

'And we've a wedding of our own to

arrange,' Jim chipped in.

'Was that our flight being called?' Caroline said suddenly as an announcement was made.

'It was,' Jim confirmed. 'Better say goodbye now, love.'

Caroline turned to Robert.

'Look after Karen for me, Bob,' she said, unable to disguise the tremor in her voice. And as their eyes met, she realised how much she cared for him still, not as a husband or in a romantic way, but as a dear friend. 'I know you will.'

Tears glinted in her eyes.

'Be happy, Bob,' she whispered, reaching up to brush his cheek with her lips.

She sensed he felt it, too — the deep affection and respect they now had for each other. And having successfully put the past behind them, they could concentrate happily on the future. Briefly they embraced.

'You be happy, too,' Bob said gruffly, then he turned to shake Jim's hand. 'Take good care of her.'

Caroline looked around for Karen. She was standing with Kate, who was obviously trying to keep her spirits high in a difficult moment.

She thought her usually confident daughter looked a little lost and out of her depth. This was, after all, the first time they'd ever been apart, let alone living on opposite sides of the world.

'Sure you're going to be OK?' Caroline asked anxiously, smoothing back a loose strand of dark hair from Karen's face. She was so lovely — this girl who was hers and Robert's . . .

'Positive,' Karen said firmly; then a tell-tale tear trickled down her cheek.

'It's just — oh, Mum, I'm going to miss you so much!'

Caroline held her daughter close, stroking her soft hair.

'Take care, darling, she murmured. 'Come home when you're ready. You know your home is with me — with Jim and me — whenever you want it.'

'I know.' Karen sniffed loudly, then laughed, embarrassed at showing her emotions. 'Sorry! I didn't mean to cry.'

'Don't be sorry, darling. It's lovely to know you care.' She dabbed at her daughter's tears.

'Remember I'm going to need you as a bridesmaid!' She tilted Karen's chin up with her finger and looked deep in her eyes.

Karen smiled through her tears.

'That's my girl!'

Caroline delved into her bag. 'Look, before I go, I have something for you. I was keeping it for your eighteenth birthday, but you may still be here and so, I'm just going to give you it now, darling.'

'What is it?' Karen's eyes shone as Caroline took a dark blue box from her bag and carefully opened it. Then she gasped with delight when she saw the gold bracelet lying against the dark blue velvet.

'Oh, Mum, it's lovely.' She held it in her fingers and the tears began to threaten again. Caroline patted her daughter's hand.

'Glad you like it, darling. Enjoy wearing it.'

Caroline looked up as Jim came towards her.

'Ready, darling?' He put his arm around her.

Caroline smiled over at Robert and Kate.

''Bye,' she called, moving towards the departure lounge. 'All the best for your wedding!'

Instinctively, Karen moved closer to her father and Kate.

Caroline stopped before they turned the corner and Jim waited while she turned back to wave for one last time, no longer making any attempt to hold back the tears.

Then she turned away quickly, and, with a brave smile at Jim, concentrated her thoughts on the long flight home.

10

The day of the wedding was glorious. The sun shone brilliantly, but a light breeze kept it cool. Inside the church, the sunlight glinted on the pews through the stained-glass windows.

From his place at the altar, Andrew smiled encouragingly at Robert. He didn't think he'd ever seen the younger man look so nervous.

Andrew had to admit to feeling a few butterflies himself.

Any pangs he felt at not being able to walk his daughter down the aisle were superceded by the pleasure he would have in marrying her to the man she loved.

Suddenly, there was a stirring at the back of the packed church and someone gestured discreetly to Andrew. He nodded at the organist and, after a brief pause, the wedding march resounded rousingly throughout the church.

And there she was.

An absolute vision in a flowing, white, satin dress, a fine, wispy veil covering her face. Everyone turned to watch Kate's slow, elegant walk down the aisle on the arm of her uncle.

Andrew couldn't hide his pride and joy on this special day.

His brother, Ted, over from Canada especially to give his favourite niece away in marriage, looked as proud as any father.

Then Robert turned slightly and stood mesmerised as Kate glided gracefully down the aisle towards him.

As she drew level with him and carefully lifted back her veil, her smile was radiant. She looked truly breathtaking. Robert thought for the umpteenth time how lucky he was to be marrying this gentle, beautiful girl.

The music drew to a close and there was a slight restless shuffling in the church.

Andrew looked around at the sea of

faces and the very special wedding service began . . .

$$\star \quad \star \quad \star$$

Karen glanced briefly at Sue's son, Greg, who'd come along to keep her company, and smiled. Then she turned her eyes back to the front of the church where her father and Kate stood before the altar.

Her dad was so tall, and good-looking, and she was bursting with happiness for him. And there was Kate, looking stunning in her satin dress.

And to think she'd have missed all this if she hadn't come to England with her mother. Her fingers strayed to the bracelet encircling her wrist and for a second, a wistful look flitted across her face as she thought of her mother and Jim.

On the other side of the church, Mrs Petrie, Andrew's elderly friend from the old folk's home, was looking splendid in her new lilac dress purchased specially for the occasion. She was sitting with Andrew's friend, Harriet Simpson, the matron of the home.

When Kate had walked past, Mrs Petrie had noted with delight that the girl was wearing the delicate, gold locket that had been a gift from her own husband so long ago.

Seeing it glinting in the sun against Kate's throat brought back to her all the happiness and love she and her husband had shared over the years until his death last year.

She was deeply touched that Kate had chosen to wear the locket that had always been so special to her.

'All right?' Harriet whispered and Mrs Petrie nodded happily. At that Harriet caught Andrew's eye and thought what a fine man he was — and how much she loved him . . .

At the same time Andrew was thinking how much he valued Harriet's support in the run-up to the wedding.

There was no doubt Kate had missed a mother's love and guidance.

Perhaps, he mused, that accounted for the slight insecurity on Kate's part that had made her attribute too much blame to Robert when Karen had suddenly appeared and changed all their lives irrevocably.

Whatever — it was all over now . . .

* * *

Robert took a deep breath and looked into Kate's trusting eyes before making his vows. It was hard to believe, at this meaningful moment, that he'd almost ruined everything, that he'd came so close to calling off the wedding and hurting Kate even more . . .

He turned to look at Andrew and the two men exchanged a look which said so much.

All through the wedding ceremony, Kate's eyes never left her father's face. She watched as he spoke, absorbing fully the meaning of each promise and vow she made.

And every time she turned to look at

the man at her side, her heart seemed to turn over with love. There were no doubts in her mind that she loved him — and that he loved her . . .

Andrew's only regret was that Alice could not be present today to see her only daughter married . . .

When the service was over, the church bells pealed merrily as Kate and Robert came out of the church to a shower of confetti and the cheers and laughter of their friends.

The reception in the marquee in the vicarage garden was almost over before Andrew managed to speak to Kate on her own. She'd been surrounded by friends and well-wishers the whole time.

'I'm glad I've caught you on your own at last, love,' he said solemnly, then his face broke into a smile and he pulled her to him in a gigantic hug. 'Did I tell you that you looked absolutely beautiful?'

'Several times, Dad!' Kate laughed. 'It's going to my head!'

'Hang on, love.' He became serious again. 'I may never have quite the same opportunity to say what I feel. You'll be off on your honeymoon soon and when you come home, well, things will be different.' He smiled again.

'Kate, I want you to know how proud I am of you. I'd never have managed all these years without you and I — '

'Dad!' Kate hugged him impulsively. 'I don't want your gratitude, your love has always been thanks enough for me. Anyway, I know it wasn't easy for you when Mum died.'

'We muddled along together though, didn't we?' He smiled. 'And now I have Harriet and, I mustn't forget dear old Sam.' He reached down to pat his faithful dog.

'It was a lovely service, Dad.' Kate touched his arm. 'You're terrific.'

★ ★ ★

In another part of the marquee, Robert had been watching Karen with young

Greg. The boy was obviously besotted with his daughter and he felt a twinge of panic.

Relax, he told himself — it was part and parcel of being a father. But he was glad when, at last, he managed to get Karen on her own.

'Kate and I will be leaving soon,' he told her gently. 'I just wanted to say goodbye before all the rush and to tell you to take care while I'm away.'

'I'll be OK, Dad. Really. Sue's nice, and I have Greg to keep me company.' Robert suppressed a smile.

'It's the best wedding I've been to,' Karen enthused. 'Kate looks beautiful. You're a lucky man! And you hardly look old enough to be my dad.'

'Flattery will get you everywhere.' Robert laughed. 'But, Karen, seriously. I'm glad of this chance to talk to you. I want you to know that I'm proud of you and I'm glad you had the courage to come looking for me.'

'You really didn't mind then?' Karen smiled.

'Mind? I'm on top of the world! Discovering that I had a daughter was like — Oh, like discovering ten vintage cars in an auction and getting the lot!'

Karen laughed at the outrageous compliment. 'Well, thank you — I think!'

'You know what I mean,' he said, his eyes shining. 'It's great being friends with your mum again after all these years, too, but you're definitely the icing on the cake, Karen.'

His expression sobered. 'Even if you do go back to Australia, we'll never lose touch, and Kate and I will be coming out to visit you.'

'That's fantastic. Thanks, Dad.' Karen reached up to kiss him. 'I longed to meet you all those years and — well, I wasn't disappointed. You're everything I dreamed you'd be and more . . . '

Robert hugged his daughter affectionately and went off in search of his beautiful, new wife.

* * *

For going on honeymoon, Kate had changed into a smart floral suit.

Outside, Robert waited to escort her to his magnificent vintage car.

He opened the door for her and she climbed into the passenger seat of the convertible, as the guests surged forward, tossing handfuls of confetti over the happy couple.

Suddenly, she remembered her bridal bouquet and stood up to toss it into the crowd.

Harriet caught it and blushed furiously when everyone cheered, then Robert started the engine. He and Kate smiled and exchanged knowing looks.

'I love you!' he said with a broad smile.

'I love you, too,' Kate whispered back.

Then Robert tooted the horn loudly and they were off on their honeymoon.

Kate looked over her shoulder, waving to Karen and her father and Harriet who was standing close to Andrew, eyes shining, clutching her flowers.

Kate smiled. She had a feeling the next wedding would indeed be Harriet's.

Then, blissfully, Kate sank back into the luxurious, leather seat, content in the knowledge that her happiness was complete.

Beside her, Robert looked proud and happy, too. Not only did he have a new wife, he had the additional pleasure of discovering he had a new daughter, too!

Yesterday was gone; from now on there would only be tomorrows.

THE END

We do hope that you have enjoyed reading this large print book.

Did you know that all of our titles are available for purchase?

We publish a wide range of high quality large print books including:
Romances, Mysteries, Classics
General Fiction
Non Fiction and Westerns

Special interest titles available in large print are:
The Little Oxford Dictionary
Music Book, Song Book
Hymn Book, Service Book

Also available from us courtesy of Oxford University Press:
Young Readers' Dictionary
(large print edition)
Young Readers' Thesaurus
(large print edition)

For further information or a free brochure, please contact us at:
Ulverscroft Large Print Books Ltd.,
The Green, Bradgate Road, Anstey,
Leicester, LE7 7FU, England.
Tel: (00 44) 0116 236 4325
Fax: (00 44) 0116 234 0205

Other titles in the
Linford Romance Library:

SECOND TIME AROUND

Margaret Mounsdon

Widowed single parent Elise Trent thought no one could replace her husband Peter, until she met policeman Mark Hampson. She is forced to seriously re-think her life when her mother-in-law Joan accepts a proposal of marriage from long time companion Seth Baxter, and her student daughter Angie and Mark's son Kyle get involved with an action group. Then Elise and Mark are further thrown together by a spate of country house burglaries . . .

SHACKLED TO THE PAST

Teresa Ashby

Midwife Laura Morgan moves in next door to Dr Steve Drake with her daughter, Abby. Steve had lost his wife and daughter when both were drowned. He becomes very fond of Abby and Laura begins to fall in love with him. But as the truth about the deaths of Steve's wife and child unfolds it seems that a happy future for them may never be possible, as long as he is haunted by the ghosts from the past.

THE BRIDE, THE BABY AND THE BEST MAN

Liz Fielding

In three weeks' time, Faith Bridges will marry safe, dependable, practical Julian. Their plans don't include children — just a nice, calm, platonic marriage. But then along comes Harry March, one adorable baby, and one cute four-year-old. Harry is definitely not safe — he's sexy, rude, impractical and utterly charming. He might have been best man material, but he isn't Faith's type at all . . . And as soon as she can stop herself kissing Harry she will tell him so!

PITCHED INTO LOVE

Judy Jarvie

Steph Baxter's invitation to her friend's Scottish castle hotel results in her having to pitch in and help out during an emergency. She's assisted by the gorgeous half-owner Jack McGregor and soon, despite business worries and his father's health, his powerful feelings for Steph take priority. But with secrets in her past, trust isn't something she can readily give. Then, as Jack's brother and wife make a re-appearance, old wounds challenge everything. Can new love survive the highland storms?